Bell Mountain

Lee Duigon

STOREHOUSE® PRESS

VALLECITO, CALIFORNIA

Published by Storehouse Press®
P.O. Box 158, Vallecito, CA 95251

Storehouse Press® is the registered trademark of Chalcedon, Inc.

Copyright © 2010 by Lee Duigon

This book is a work of fiction. Names, characters, businesses, organizations, places, events, and incidents either are the product of the author's imagination or used fictitiously. Any resemblance to actual persons, living or dead, events, or locales is entirely coincidental.

All rights reserved, including the right of reproduction in whole or in part in any form.

Book design by Kirk DouPonce (www.DogEaredDesign.com)

Printed in the United States of America

First Edition

Library of Congress Catalog Card Number: 2009943824

ISBN-13: 978-1-891375-52-1

ISBN-10: 1-891375-52-0

CHAPTER 1

Jack Has a Dream

This is a story about a boy who was so haunted by a mountain that it gave him bad dreams. You may have had bad dreams when you were Jack's age, but not like these.

In Jack's dream, he would be somewhere in the valley, maybe trying to throw a stone across the river. Where Jack lived, the Imperial River ran quick and cold, sparkling and chuckling, over a rocky bed with stones worn smooth as eggs. Lush green grass like a carpet, spattered with tiny purple flowers, grew right up to the water's edge. And the mountains towered over it; for Jack lived in a valley.

So he would be throwing stones, or looking for blackberries, all by himself as usual, when suddenly the mountain would begin to sing.

It was always the biggest mountain, Bell Mountain, with its peak hidden in a cloak of clouds so that no one ever saw it. Jack had never in his life heard the sound of a really big bell, or he might have said the mountain rang, not sang.

But it was a terrible song that made the other mountains tremble and filled the whole valley as if God had flooded it to the foothills with ice water. Jack couldn't hear the noise of the river anymore, nor the wind, the birds, nor his own heart beating. Indeed, it seemed the river stopped flowing and his heart stopped beating. And he was too terrified to pick up his feet and run away—too terrified even to breathe.

And then he would wake up.

As his breath came back to him, he would always find that he was still frightened: scared enough to shiver. But on top of being frightened, and running deeper than the fear, was something else.

He would always catch himself straining his ears to hear more—hungry for more, thirsty for more, more of the mountain's singing.

"Jack! Burn you for a lazy imp—wake up and get busy."

That was Van, Jack's stepfather. Jack's father, Vill, died in a war when Jack was just a baby. His mother was dead now, too, leaving him all alone with Van, who would just as soon not have him.

"I'm coming," Jack said, and crawled off the pallet he slept on. It was stuffed with ferns and moss and leaves, and it crackled every time he moved.

"I have to go down to Caristun today. His honor the chief has bought some new furniture." Van was a carter. He worked for the village council. "I want you to clean up around here. I'm tired of looking at a mess. And bring in another load of firewood. Too cuss't cold at night for this time of year."

As if he could go to Caristun and back in one day, Jack thought. He'd need a magic chariot for that—not a creaking old cart with a single bad-tempered ox to pull it.

Van was just finishing up his breakfast and packing some buttered bread in his scrip to eat along the way. He was a short, stubby man with a stubby black beard and stubby black hairs on his arms and hands.

Jack couldn't remember his father and had never seen a picture of him. Mother said he looked like his father. He remembered her as a frail, pretty lady, never in the best of health: lying in her bed for half a year, promising to get better, and finally dying there. Whatever made her decide to marry Van?

Jack was not frail, and he was already getting almost as tall as Van. He had his mother's eyes, deep blue, and a shock of glossy black hair, which she used to say was like Vill's hair. Poor Vill, who went marching out with a spear on his shoulder, singing, and never came back. He lay buried a little north of Lintum Forest, where the raiders killed him.

"There's some tack in the shed that needs seeing to," Van said. "I don't suppose you've done it yet."

"I'll do it before you get back."

"It ain't like I pile work on you. Little enough you have to do to earn your keep. There's kids your age as is already let out to be shepherds, and that's what they have to do all day, every day—until the Heathen get 'em, or outlaws, or some wolves. You could at least do your chores."

Whenever Van grumbled like this, it meant he was ready to leave and just putting it off for another minute or two. Lately he grumbled a lot when he had to go as far as Caristun. Jack never talked back to him. Getting hit by Van would hurt, but it wasn't fear of getting hit that made Jack behave. He knew somehow that Van would love it if he gave him some sass, and an excuse to beat him. He knew Van hated it when he acted as if he respected him—hated it and couldn't find a way to punish him for it.

"I'm off," Van said, snatching his hat and cloak from the peg on the wall. "Mind you do your chores."

Jack did do his chores and would have liked it better if he'd had more of them. Van was proud of his home—a four-room cottage, each room smaller than the next—but as small as it was, it didn't take a lot of cleaning. Van always wanted the plaster and the floors kept clean in case he had company.

Most of the houses in the village of Ninneburky were just as small. The village itself was more than grand enough to be a town: a real town, with an archon and a seat on the Oligarchy. It had more people and newer and better buildings than the town of Caristun, to whose archon the village paid dues.

One thing Caristun had, which Ninneburky didn't have, that made all the difference—a wall of dressed stone to defend it. Ninneburky made do with a stockade of timber. There was nothing quite so costly these days (Van said) as a defensive wall, what with stonecutters, masons, laborers, the stone itself, and the cost of getting it there. Ninneburky might have its own new Chamber of the Temple, lovely fine houses for all the members of the council, a livery stable, and a militia that drilled with spears, with a real sergeant to instruct them—but it did not yet have a wall of stone. The chief councilor swore he'd build a wall and be an archon, or die trying. To that end the dues on craftsmen, loggers, shopkeepers, carters, marketers, and herdsmen were rather high. Jack knew because Van complained about it frequently.

In the afternoon he went to the chamber to see his teacher, Ashrof. Jack used to go to him to be taught his letters. The old man was Mother's great-uncle, and Jack had had to promise her that he'd see him. She was the only family Ashrof had in Ninneburky.

Jack didn't think there was a word for "your mother's great-uncle." But after Mother died, Jack came to think of the old man as the only family he had—more family than Van would ever be, at least. Besides, Ashrof had more to teach than letters.

Jack saw him come out of the chamber building with another one of his pupils—the stuck-up little stink who was the chief councilor's daughter. The chamber was going to open a regular school soon, where all the children who needed to learn their letters could learn them at the same time, probably from someone younger than Ashrof. Until then, Ashrof taught those who came to him.

Jack stopped and the girl walked right past him as if he weren't there at all: didn't even look at him. For two bits he'd trip her. Then she'd look.

"Bucket! What's the matter?"

Jack's mother called him Bucket as a pet name. She said it was the first word he learned how to say, after "Ma-ma," and he used to say it so much that it'd make her laugh. Now Ashrof called him Bucket. No one else did. Jack turned and joined him by the bench next to the chamber door.

"That girl makes me want to stick a moth up her nose," Jack said.

"Poor Ellayne!" Ashrof said. But his white beard jiggled, which meant he was chuckling under it. He dropped himself on the bench and patted the boards. "Sit down by me a while. The day's finally warmed up enough to enjoy a bit of sun.

"You mustn't mind Ellayne. Her mother wants her to grow up to be a great lady in Obann, an archon's daughter. Her father would sell his soul to go to Obann and be the archon—but he hates the very thought of his daughter living there. It will never be possible for Ellayne to please both her mother and her father."

"She acts like I'm not here," Jack said.

"Her head has been filled with a great deal of foolishness," Ashrof said. "Now how about your head, eh?"

"I know what you mean. Yes, I had the dream again last night. Why won't it go away? Whoever heard of having dreams about a mountain? A mountain's just there. It doesn't matter."

"*King Ozias said, I shall hang a bell atop Mount Yul, and when it shall be rungen, maybe the Lord shall hear. And Penda the prophet said, He shall surely hear.*"

Ashrof had his eye on the mountain now, Bell Mountain. It seemed he was reciting the words not to Jack, but to the mountain. Bell Mountain, with its rocky shoulders, its snowy shields gleaming as the sun began to decline westward, and the perpetual clouds that masked its crown—it towered over the valley. Anyone in town could simply look up and see it. Until he'd started having the dreams, Jack never gave it a thought. It was just there. It had nothing to do with anything in his life.

"What was that you said?" Jack asked.

"A bit of Scripture—the real Scripture, from the Old Books." Ashrof continued to study the mountain. "Not much call for the Old Books nowadays. There are presters who have never read them.

"But I have. I knew there was something about your dream that reminded me of a verse I used to know long ago. It took me a long time to find that verse.

"It's from the Record of Penda, 50th fascicle, verse 16: the part that tells how the last rightful king of Obann, King Ozias, had to flee his refuge in the forest—the one we still call Oziah's Wood. How some of his followers betrayed him to his enemies. They thought he'd try to make for Lintum Forest because he was born there; but he tricked them again. He went up the mountain, which in those days was called Mount Yul, or Mount Cloud." He pointed to the mountain and finally looked back down at Jack.

"The Scripture doesn't say whether he ever got to the top of the mountain and put a bell up there. No one ever saw him again, dead or alive. And after him there were no more kings. Just the long years of the Interregnum, out of which arose the Empire—God forgive us!"

Jack didn't know how to answer. Ashrof had taught him a little about some of these things. He knew there was an Empire, with the city of Obann as its capital, a very, very long time ago. And that the Old Books of Scripture were even older than the Empire. That was about all he knew.

"Why did you say 'God forgive us'?"

"Because the Empire was hopelessly corrupt and wicked, and God destroyed it," Ashrof said. "Obann's Empire ruled the world. Up and down the coast of the Great Sea, and many islands far out to sea. Down to the deserts of the south, and far to the north, well beyond the River Winter. Wasn't so cold up there in those days. And way out east beyond the mountains. Obann conquered all the Heathen lands out to the Great Lakes. It was a bigger world then, Bucket, and the whole world did homage to the Empire.

"But God destroyed it, all in one day, the Day of Fire foretold by all the prophets. Nobody knew what they meant, you see. There was no Empire yet, while the prophets were alive, and wouldn't be for hundreds of years. So no one believed, and no one listened. Nevertheless, God did destroy the Empire, leaving nothing but ruins to this day."

"Why did God do that?"

"I told you—because it was wicked and corrupt, and merciless," said Ashrof. "And now you come along with your dream about Bell Mountain. I find it very troubling!"

He had to explain to Jack that a bell was like a great bronze cup that, when struck, could be heard for miles around. "Just the same as if you clanked a tin cup with your knife, only thousands of times greater. There are bells in Obann City, which they ring for special occasions—when the oligarchs vote to go to war or the First Prester dies.

"Well, if someone rang a great bell from the top of Bell Mountain, it might well seem that the mountain itself was singing. And the other mountains all around would catch the sound and magnify it so that it filled the whole valley. That'd be a rather terrifying sound, especially if you'd never heard the like of it before. I think it'd be just like the sound you hear in your dream."

"But why should I dream that!" Jack cried.

"I don't know, my boy. I burn'd well don't know." Ashrof suddenly shook his head, like a dog shaking off water, and hugged himself. "Stinking cold last night, though, eh? I find this sun today doesn't quite warm me as it should.

"Come back again tomorrow, Bucket. I really must have time to think on this. And pray."

CHAPTER 2

The Councilor's Daughter

Chief Councilor Roshay Bault, Ellayne's father, lived in a fine house with all the bedrooms on the second story and a carved oak stairway to get you there and back. Van's whole house would have fit in the formal room and the parlor without encroaching on the kitchen, dining room, and the rest of the ground floor. But because Ellayne had lived in it all her life, she didn't see anything wonderful about it.

It seemed much less than wonderful just now because she was listening to her mother and father wrangle over her. They were at it when she came home from the chamber house, and didn't hear her come in, or they would have stopped. Ellayne stood in the hall listening as they argued in the parlor.

"The girls' school in the city is a perfectly respectable place, and we can well afford it now," her mother said. "She'll be with girls from the best families in the land, and it will advance her more than anything we could possibly do for her in this place." Ellayne's mother, tall and thin, had a reedy voice that carried a long way, like notes played on a human flute.

"How many times do I have to tell you, Vannett? The answer is no!" That was her father's bass drum voice, the one he used at council meetings when he had to raise the dues.

"Those girls from the best families will only laugh at her. Their fathers are archons, or at least related to archons."

"Pooh! We can buy and sell half of them. They won't laugh at our wealth."

"That's exactly what they will be laughing at!"

"Do you mean to keep her here in this miserable village forever, Roshay? Learning her letters from a doddering old fool who should've been put out to pasture years ago! And someday marry her off to a shepherd, or a cotter, or a cobbler?"

There was a great deal more of it, some of which Ellayne didn't understand, but all of which made her feel like kicking her new shoes off and throwing them down a well. It used to make her cry, but she'd learned how to stifle that.

She crept to the kitchen and out the back door. The cook and the maid were busy in the kitchen and pretended to be too busy to notice her. The cook used to give her treats, but didn't anymore. Ellayne passed them and went outside through the back door.

She used to watch her brothers in the yard playing with sticks, dueling: playing outlaws. They were too old for that now, and too old for her. Dib spent most of his time now handling bits of business for Father, this deal or that. And Josek went from town to town doing politics. Ellayne didn't see much of them anymore.

For no reason at all, she thought of the boy she saw on the street as she was leaving the chamber house today. She'd seen him before. He was probably one of Ashrof's pupils, like her. Only his clothes were so shabby it was hard to imagine why he'd need to know how to read and write, or how his family could pay for the lessons.

Well, whatever his life is like, she thought, it's sure to be more fun than mine. When his lessons were over, he probably ran out to the fields to play with his friends. They'd be stalking one another through the woods, exploring ruins, or splashing around one of the fords in the river. Playing outlaws, probably.

Ellayne was allowed to do none of these things. She used to be; but now she was old enough, her mother said, to have to behave like a chief councilor's daughter.

She wished her father were a cobbler. Then maybe she might have friends.

Jack went out to the riverbank, but he did not play. With the mountain peering over his shoulder everywhere he went, he tried to remember what Ashrof had taught him about the Old Books and the ancient times.

"Your mother charged me to teach you the Scriptures," Ashrof often said. "Someday, we hope, you'll read well enough to read the Old Books for yourself. There aren't many who do nowadays."

Of course, Jack was too young to learn a lot of history and doctrine. He was much too young to be told that the Temple didn't like people reading the Scriptures, much less teaching them to boys, and that Ashrof would have gotten into a great deal of trouble for doing so.

This was why Ashrof had been so careful in his teaching, playing it out in little dribs and drabs. Because of that, Jack was in a muddle about it. He knew that there were good kings in Obann once, in the beginning, who were faithful to God and defended the people from their enemies; and that the kings, and then the people themselves, over time went bad; and that when the last kings tried to turn back to God again, it was too late. Jack knew the Old Books were full of battles and prophecies and miracles and holy wisdom, but he didn't know enough to make sense of any of it. He pondered it until his head hurt.

He went home still in a muddle, made his supper, and went to bed. And as he lay down in the dark and his pallet rustled and crumpled under him, an extraordinary thought took hold of him, and he sat up in bed.

"What would happen if someone climbed to the top of the mountain and rang that bell?" he said to himself. "He could scare the living daylights out of everyone in the valley!"

He pictured the people of Ninneburky scurrying through the streets like ants when you turn over a log and uncover their nest. They wouldn't know what to do! Jack couldn't imagine what they would do. And there were other towns around the valley, more ants' nests to stir up.

He could not have told you why, but to ring that bell was now the one thing he wanted to do more than anything in all the world.

CHAPTER 3

A Truth That Can't Be Told

Jack woke up early, not sure he'd really slept at all—but not a bit tired either. He meant to do his chores after breakfast, but it was no use. His head was too full of the mountain to bother with chores.

He arrived at the chamber house so early that the sexton had to go down the street and call Ashrof away from his breakfast. The old man came huffing and puffing, huddled in his cloak against the chill. You could see his breath.

"Jack! What's the matter? Why are you here so early? Is something wrong?"

"I didn't know you started your day so late, nuncle." That was a word used in Obann to address an older man whom one was fond of. "Listen—I'm going to climb the mountain."

"Oh, what are you talking about? Let's go inside. It's too cold out here for these old bones. Cusset unseasonable weather!"

In addition to its great hall for worship ceremonies and the like, the chamber house contained many smaller rooms for all sorts of purposes. Ashrof had a classroom, which would someday be filled with stools and given to a younger man who could teach many children at once. It had one bare wall, painted black, upon which the teacher could write in chalk. It was dark, and Ashrof had to light a lamp. It was also cold, but there was little he could do about that.

"Now sit down and make some sense," he said, pushing Jack toward a stool. "What's this about climbing a mountain?"

Jack's mind was racing. He'd have to slow down and help Ashrof catch up.

"Bell Mountain," he said. "You told me about it yesterday, remember?"

"Well, yes, of course. But why should anybody climb it?"

"To ring the bell. The bell that God can hear. I'm going to ring the bell on Bell Mountain."

"Ho-ho-ho!" Ashrof jiggled on his stool. "You had me called away from my oatmeal for that?"

If Jack had had more adults to talk to—Van never listened—he might've become angry with Ashrof for refusing to take him seriously. But he only thought the old man hadn't caught up with him yet.

"I'm going to ring the bell that King Ozias put on top of the mountain," Jack said. "I want you to tell me how to get up there and what'll happen when God hears the bell."

Ashrof stared hard at him for a long time. Jack waited for his answer.

"My boy, you mustn't think of such things," Ashrof said at last.

"Why not?"

"Well—well, for one thing, no one's ever climbed that mountain."

"You said King Ozias did!"

"Bucket, nobody climbs those mountains! It's hard enough just getting over the passes, as the raiders and the traders do. Nobody climbs to the top. It may not even be possible."

"But you said King Ozias—"

Ashrof held up his hand. "No! The Scripture says Ozias intended to climb the mountain. That's where he said he was going, before he and the last of his men disappeared forever. We are not told whether he got there."

But Jack had already thought of that.

"You said he was talking to a prophet. The prophet would've told him if he wasn't going to make it. But all the prophet said was that God would hear the bell if someone rang it. He wouldn't have said that if there wasn't going to be a bell."

Ashrof winced. He shivered in his cloak. Jack couldn't imagine what was wrong with him, aside from being cold.

"Jack, listen to me. You can't go to the top of Bell Mountain and ring Ozias' bell any more than you could walk across the tops of the waves from Caha to the mainland like the Children of Geb."

"Who?"

"They were faithful to God, so He saved them when He sank Caha into the depths of the sea. He made them able to walk on the water. But don't you see? The Old Books are full of miracles, but nobody walks on water anymore. The Books tell us about times long ago. The Empire was a thousand years ago, but King Ozias was a thousand years before that. There are no Books of Scripture since Ozias' time. We have no record of any miracles since then."

Jack had not expected this. What was wrong with Ashrof? "Nuncle, don't you believe the things you teach me? You sound like you don't believe there is a bell."

"No, no, that's not it! Of course I believe—I must believe!" Ashrof took a deep breath. "But it's not so simple as you think, Bucket.

"If you tried to climb that mountain, you would surely die. Either you'd fall, or some wild beast would get you, or you'd freeze to death when you got to the snows. Besides which, how could Ozias have dragged a great bell up there in the first place?"

"So the Scriptures aren't true?" Jack cried.

"No, no, no! I'm not saying that. I would never say that. It's just that God often speaks to us in riddles. That's why no one ever believed any of the prophecies when they were made. No one understands a prophecy until after it has come true. Only then can they see what the prophet meant.

"Jack, there are truths that can't be told by plain speaking. They can only be told in a roundabout way, by telling stories that point to a higher truth. These are called symbols. Ozias' bell is a symbol—a way of talking about something else in a way that people can remember it. The truth of the story is that God will hear the people when they cry out to Him."

"You just said it with plain speaking," Jack said. "You never said anything about symbols or whatnot."

Ashrof gave him a pained look. "I was saving that for when you were older," he said. "It takes a long time to understand such things as the symbols found in Scripture. You haven't lived long enough for that."

If Jack had been able to read the Scriptures on his own, he might have known of a verse spoken by King Ozias when he was trying to lead the people back to God: *Babes and children see what is hidden from you in your foolish wisdom.* But he didn't know the verse, and it seemed to him that Ashrof was talking a lot of mush and wasn't going to help.

"So you see, it would be foolish to climb the mountain and expect to find a bell up there," Ashrof said. "That's not what the Scripture really means. If it were, don't you think I'd want to climb the mountain with you?"

Jack didn't think so. For the first time in his life, he had a glimmer of what it might mean to grow old. A young Ashrof, he thought, would already be packing a kit for the climb.

"I'll climb it alone, nuncle," he said. "I'll climb to the top and ring King Ozias' bell, and God will hear it. I want to see what He does."

"Haven't you understood a word I've said?" Ashrof cried.

"You don't believe the story you taught me from the Scripture," Jack said. "Well, I'm going to find out if it's true. When you hear the bell, you'll find out, too."

Jack got up and left, although Ashrof tried to keep him. There was nothing to be gained by listening to any more of his symbols.

One thing Jack knew for sure, and there was nothing that Ashrof could say against it. He'd dreamed about the bell for months before Ashrof told him the story from the Scriptures. The mountain had called, and he would come. He wouldn't let anyone stop him.

CHAPTER 4

Van's Fish Story

Van came home that evening in such a state that he forgot to chide Jack about his chores. Jack didn't mind getting his supper for him, and for once Van seemed grateful for it.

"I don't think I've ever been so happy to see a mug of ale in all my life," he said when Jack placed one before him. He took a long drink and then slumped in his chair with his hat still on the table. Jack hung it up for him.

"I don't know what people think who never go farther than the end of the valley," he said, "but I'll tell you one thing. If you go as far as Caristun, you'll see a few things that'll make you wonder. And hear a few, too!"

He'd made an early start for Caristun, and the ox pulled with a steady pace. "And it was all day warming up," he said.

But he'd had to make a stop where Oziah's Wood came closest to the opposite bank of the river.

"There were some fishermen, and one of 'em sang out to me to stop. So I did. 'Carter!' he says. 'If you've got room in your cart, have we got a haul for you! Come and see.'

"So I come up to where they were gathered round, and what do you think they had? A fish, so help me, burn'd near as big as the cart! 'Well, that's some fishing you boys have done,' I says. 'What the blessing kind of fish d'you call that? I swear I never saw the like of it.'

"'Nor have we, my lad,' says the eldest of 'em—a real greybeard. 'He's made a mess of our net, too. I've been fishing this stretch of the river all my days, and I have never seen a fish like this. Never!'

"So I asked him, 'Is it good or bad?' And he says it depends on if they can sell it for enough to make up for the net. He don't know who'll buy a fish you might not be able to eat. 'Been a few strange things in the water lately,' he says. 'About a mile from here in a little creek where I go to catch crawfish for bait, I almost caught something that might've caught me.' And he told me about it. 'You ever see any of them little sally-manders what lives under rocks and logs? Well, try to imagine one as big as your forearm with a head as big as your fist; and nasty, pale, flabby skin; and jaws a-snappin', looking to bite the fingers off your hand. I was so surprised, I fell right on my keister. When I got up again, it was gone.'"

They wanted Van to haul the great fish into town for them and paid him a penny to do it. It took all five fishermen to wrestle it into the cart. They knew people would have to see it or they wouldn't believe them. And to be sure, there was no one else in Caristun who'd ever seen a fish like that. The men were trying to sell it when Van left them to pick up the chief's furniture.

Jack served Van bread and sausages and an onion from their store. As he wolfed it down, he continued the story of his trip.

At the inn where he spent the night in Caristun, the talk around the fireplace was all about unsettling news from near and far.

"Up north, toward the River Winter, farmers have been pulling up stakes and heading south, and there aren't many farmers up there to begin with," Van said. "They've been telling all kinds of wild stories about monsters in the woods.

"Out west, where the river gets lost in the North and South Mires before it finds the sea, people have seen lights moving around the mires by night. No one dares to traipse around there by day—too easy to get sucked down. There's otter and muskrat trappers who go there, but they say they wouldn't dare go out at night. They've been having good hauls of furs, but they don't like some of the noises they've been hearing lately."

The general opinion of all the travelers was that the world was getting strange and scary, never mind what the presters from the Temple said.

The worst news came from the east, from the hills and forests that lapped up against the mountains, where miners and loggers worked.

"There's going to be a war, that's certain," Van said. "A regular, all-out war with armies. The Heathen are fixing to come over the mountains by the thousands. That's why there hasn't been much raiding this year. They're busy building up their strength for an invasion, so they can hit us hard. Won't be long before the Big Bosses in Obann start making ready for it."

He shook his head and sighed, and drained the rest of his ale.

"I didn't see anything funny on the way home," he said. "But just before I come within hailing distance of the stockade, as I was passing by that little patch of woods, I heard something. A lot of whistling, like—only it didn't sound like birds. I'll swear it wasn't birds. Pour me another mug of ale, Jack. I reckon I'm lucky to be back—with the furniture I fetched for the chief, much good may it do him!"

CHAPTER 5

A Stuck-Up Girl and an Ignorant Boy

On days when he didn't have to travel out of town, Van would report to the council stables for whatever work they had for him. Any of the councilors could call on him to transport this or that, either on the cart or on his back.

Having caught up on his chores, Jack would ordinarily have gone off to amuse himself—by the riverbank, in the meadows, with other boys or alone. It was usually alone. The other boys had fathers and mothers. They weren't waiting for a stepfather to find a new wife, have children of his own, and get rid of an unwanted stepson. Van's own son, once he had one, would get his cart and his job. Jack would be lucky if Van didn't hire him out to a caravan or as a servant to a logging gang.

He didn't have to go beyond the stockade to see the mountain. Bell Mountain loomed in the east, mocking Jack's dreams with its silence. He would have liked to have had the dream again last night, but it didn't come. What would he do if it never came again?

"When are you going?"

Jack jumped, startled by the voice behind him. How

long he'd been standing by Van's tack shed, gazing up at the mountain, he never knew.

He came down with his hair standing on end on the back of his neck, fists balled—and was even madder when he saw who it was.

"What are you doing here?" he snapped. "Who do you think you are, sneaking up on me like that!"

It was the girl from the chamber house, the stuck-up one, the councilor's daughter. She had her golden hair in braids. She wore a dress that was cleaner than anything Jack had ever owned and shiny new shoes.

"What are you doing here!" he said.

"I followed you from the chamber house yesterday. I was in the hallway, right outside the classroom, and you charged right past and never saw me."

"Is that so?"

"You needn't be snotty," she said. "I came for my lessons, and I heard you and Ashrof talking, and you said you were going to climb Bell Mountain. Are you?"

"What business is it of yours? I don't even know your name." He did know, but he was too angry to remember it.

"It's Ellayne. My father is Roshay Bault, the chief councilor. I know your name. It's Jack Bucket. Silly name!"

For two spits Jack would have knocked her down, but he knew boys didn't hit girls—especially girls whose fathers were councilors. Van would sell him to the Heathen for a human sacrifice if he hit this girl.

"What I do is no business of yours, Miss Busybody," he said. "And nobody said you could come into this yard. So get lost!"

"I will not get lost," Ellayne said. "I won't go until you

tell me all about the mountain, and the bell, and all the rest. I heard some of it yesterday, but not all. And I wasn't snooping. I couldn't help hearing it."

"You must have mush for brains. Why should I tell you anything at all?"

She stood as stiff as a militia captain on parade and said, "Because I really want to know! I'd tell you if you asked me. I don't think Ashrof even wanted to hear it, but you told him."

Jack didn't play with councilors' children and didn't know what they were like. Maybe this one was the best of the lot. But very few people can pass up an invitation to talk about themselves and their plans, and Jack wasn't one of them.

"Why not?" he said. He kicked an old keg that lay on the ground beside him. "Sit here." And he sat on a piece of a log that he was saving for firewood in the winter. It gave him some pleasure to see how careful she had to be of her dress when she sat on the keg.

"All right, then—what do you want to know?"

"You're really going to climb Bell Mountain? All the way up?"

"I'm really going to do it."

"To ring the bell?"

"You bet."

"But Ashrof said you'd never get up the mountain. It's too dangerous. You'll fall, or get eaten by a bear, or freeze to death."

Jack laughed. She really had been listening yesterday.

"Don't be silly," he said. "If it was impossible to get to the top of the mountain, there wouldn't be a bell up there."

"But how do you know there even is a bell?" Ellayne

said. "That's what I don't get. Ashrof doesn't think there's a bell."

Jack's chin tilted up a little without him knowing it.

"Oh, there's a bell up there, all right," he said. "I know."

"How? How do you know?"

"Because a long time before Ashrof ever told me about it, I dreamed of it. That's how I know."

Ellayne asked a hundred questions, and Jack answered them. He didn't like her, but he liked talking about the bell. The keg and the log got to be uncomfortable by and by, so he asked her into the house, and they sat at Van's table. She darted glances all around like she'd never been in a house before. He couldn't know that Ellayne's house was so fine and roomy inside that Van's place was a wonder to her. He would've stared just as she did, had he been inside her house—staring at walls that were painted and regularly scrubbed clean. Van's walls were bare plaster, stained with smoke.

They'd just about talked themselves out when Ellayne again brought up the subject of the danger.

"Oh, I've already heard all about that," Jack said. "Everything outside the stockade is dangerous, to hear Van tell it." And he told her about Van's trip to Caristun. That story seemed to get under her skin.

"It reminds me of something else I've heard about," she said. "The last time my father was in Obann City, just before the winter, there was a reciter from the Temple who'd gone all balmy in the head. He was marching up and down the street in a filthy robe, with ashes on his head, yelling at the top of his lungs about the wrath of God and the world coming to an end. Everybody dropped what they were doing to listen to him. You couldn't help but listen, my father said. He said it was like having icicles grow down your back. Until finally a couple of guards from the Temple came and hauled him off, and that was that. The First Prester really doesn't like that kind of talk, my father says. He wouldn't be surprised if they put that reciter in a dungeon and cut his tongue out."

Jack tried to imagine Ashrof doing a thing like that, but couldn't.

"I wonder what made him do it," he said.

"Who knows? My father said a lot of the people on the street nodded their heads, agreeing with the madman. Well, that's Obann for you, he says."

Ellayne leaned across the table. "After I heard you and Ashrof talking, and thought about it all day," she said, "I remembered that man.

"What if it was true—what he said, about God being angry and the world coming to an end? And what if there really is a bell on the mountain? What if God's been waiting all this time for someone to ring it? If I were God and if there was a bell that people were supposed to ring so I would hear it, I guess I'd be pretty mad if they never rang it, not once. Do you see?"

Jack nodded. He did see, or at least he saw dimly. "It'd be like forgetting God, wouldn't it?" he said. "No wonder He's angry."

"That's why I came here!" Ellayne said. "I had to find out if you were really going to try to ring the bell. Because if you are, I'm coming with you."

It took a moment for that to sink in. Jack thought he'd never heard anything so outrageous in his whole life.

"You must be crazier than I thought!" he said. "Why

under the sky would I want to take you with me? A girl! I suppose you'd climb the mountain in that dress and in those shiny shoes!"

She smacked her palms on the table, making it jump.

"You really are the most ignorant boy I've ever met!" she said. "I'd wear boys' clothes, stupid! And boots. And I'd have you cut off my hair so I could be disguised as another boy. Nobody but you would know the difference.

"And anyhow, I've got something you don't have and that we'll need if we're going to get anywhere."

"Oh! And what's that?" Jack sneered.

Ellayne grinned at him.

"Money!" she said.

CHAPTER 6

How to Have Adventures

In all his life Jack had never been more than a mile or two away from his hometown and had never been taught about maps or geography. He could see the mountain from his own backyard. All he had to do, he thought, was to keep on walking toward it until he got there, and then somehow climb it. He thought it might take a day or two to get there and maybe another day for the climb. Had he been left alone to act on such notions, he surely would have come to grief.

"You're lucky I came along. You don't know anything," Ellayne said, when they met in secret the next day. The first thing they decided to do was to keep it secret that they knew each other. Neither Ellayne's parents nor Van would have dreamed of letting them play together—not that they were playing. This was serious business. So today they met in Van's tack shed, Jack having hung a rag from the doorpost to let Ellayne know Van wasn't home.

"There aren't any roads to Bell Mountain," she told him. "The only people who ever get close to the mountain are loggers, and they float everything up and down the river. With all the time they lose hauling things around the shallow places, it takes a week.

"Besides, you don't go straight up the mountain. You can't. When you can't go by the river anymore, there are the foothills, and they're all in thick forest. No roads there! Before you got anywhere near the mountain, you'd first have to get through the forest."

"How do you know so much about it?" Jack said.

"My father has money in logging. My brother Dib has been all the way up the river several times. They talk about it over supper."

"Oh."

"But we can't go up the river, anyhow," Ellayne said. "Sooner or later my father will know I've run away, and Van'll know you're gone, and they'll come looking for us. Father will turn out the militia. If we go up the river, someone's bound to see us and we'll probably be caught. So we have to find another way."

"Van won't bother to come after me," Jack said.

"They'll figure it out that we're together. My father's not stupid. He'll be after both of us."

"So which way should we go, then?"

Long ago in Obann there used to be roads to take people almost anywhere they wished to go and books that listed all the towns along the roads and the distances between them. There were no such books anymore; the cities listed in them were ruins, and time had erased most of the roads. As for maps, no one between the mountains and the sea had made a map in hundreds of years. Neither Jack nor Ellayne had ever seen one. So although Ellayne knew much more than Jack, she didn't know much.

"We'll have to go by a roundabout way," she said. "We'll either have to go north of the river, or south."

"We'd meet too many people going north," Jack said. He knew from Van that the lands between the Imperial

River and the Chariot River were full of farmers and herdsmen, with loggers in Oziah's Wood and some villages too small to have stockades.

"South's better," Ellayne agreed. "If we can get to Lintum Forest without being stopped, we'll have a good chance of going all the way."

"Lintum Forest—King Ozias was born there!" Jack said. "I forgot that. Well, that is the way we ought to go! It's King Ozias' bell we want to find. It'll bring us good luck to go through Lintum Forest. How far is it?"

Ellayne didn't know. Her brothers never went there. "There are outlaws in it," she said. "I've heard that much."

"If there are outlaws there, that means it's a good place to go to avoid getting caught."

———

The next day they met, Ellayne brought along a bulky package that turned out to be a book—the first one Jack had ever seen, not counting the books at the chamber house. Thanks to Ashrof's teaching, he was able to read the letters burned onto the leather cover.

"*The Mem ... Mem-o-ire of Abombalbap,*" he read. "What in the blazes is that?"

"It's a book about how to have adventures," Ellayne said. "My father used to read this to me at bedtime, and now I can read it for myself, so he gave it to me. My mother doesn't think these are the right kind of stories for girls."

"How can this help us?"

"Abombalbap was the rightful heir to a castle long ago. His stepmother wanted to kill him when he was still a baby, so she gave him to a shepherd to feed to the wolves. But the shepherd kept him alive instead, and raised him. When he was old enough, he traveled all around having adventures until he found out who he really was and got his castle back."

Jack had never heard of anything like that. "What's a castle?" he said.

"It's a place sort of like the Prester's Palace in Obann. It has high walls and towers and a moat around it. There used to be lots of castles in the old days.

"Abombalbap had adventures with bandits, and Heathen raiders, and robber lords, giants, dwarfs, magicians—and he always came out on top. The book tells you how he did it."

Jack picked up the book. "We can't take this with us. It weighs too much."

"I know that!" Ellayne snapped. "I'm just showing it to you to prove I know all about adventures."

Had they known better what lay ahead of them, Jack and Ellayne would have planned much more carefully, or else given up the idea altogether. But they didn't know, and they wanted to leave soon, so they planned accordingly. If they ran into trouble, Ellayne said, they would just do whatever Abombalbap did when he was in difficulties.

She cut open the lining of her coat and hid money in it, wrapping it so it wouldn't jingle—a trick she'd learned from the book. Jack was amazed when he saw the money.

"You've got so much more money than Van—and he's a grown man who gets paid a penny a day. You didn't steal it from your father, did you?" he said. She had silver pennies, threepenny pips, fivepenny moons, and something he'd never seen in Van's possession—three gold pieces, newly minted "spears" (so called for the image they bore of a spearman standing at attention).

"Of course I didn't steal it!" Ellayne said. "My mother and father give me an allowance, and I save it. I was going to buy a horse and carriage when they said I was old enough to have one. It ought to be enough to get us to the mountain and back. We'll need to buy food and lots of other things."

They'd need sturdy boots, she said, and warm clothes for Jack and fur bags to sleep in, like the loggers had. They'd have to buy them in another town—too risky to buy them here, where people would notice and tell her father.

"We'll want to buy weapons, too," she added. "Bows and arrows for hunting for food along the way, and swords and knives—just in case."

Jack could only marvel. She really did know all about adventures, and she was going to spend all her money on theirs. Van would never buy him boots. He felt as if they were all but on the mountain already.

"Don't tell me you know how to use a bow and arrows," he said.

"We can learn. I can ride a horse, though."

He shook his head, dazzled. "I can get us rabbits and woodchucks with my slingshot," he said. "We won't go hungry. I can cook them, too. But I never thought of any of the rest. I had you figured all wrong. Now I'm glad you're going with me—you really do know what you're doing. I can hardly wait to get started! How about tomorrow morning, first thing?"

Ellayne wanted to make it the day after: she needed time to get some things together. "We'll both need to carry packs," she said, "with everything in them that we'll need.

I'm sure there are some clothes of my brothers' that'll fit you, and I'll need some of their things, too. Maybe you ought to pack some cooking gear. And don't forget your slingshot."

CHAPTER 7

The Journey Begins

Jack didn't think that day would ever come. He was sure something would go wrong. Van would hurt himself on the job, and Jack would have to stay home and tend to him; Ellayne's father would find out; or Ashrof would decide to tell on him because he was sure Jack would come to a bad end if no one stopped him.

He would have liked to say good-bye to Ashrof and ask the old reciter for his blessing. He knew the priest at the chamber house didn't like Ashrof, thought he was too old and foolish. Jack would have been happier with Ashrof's blessing, but knew he'd have to do without it. He could make it up with him when he came back.

He stuffed a canvas sack with two small pans, two knives and two forks, his slingshot, some bread, some onions, and what little spare clothing he had. It didn't seem like much. He found an old wineskin that would serve for holding water.

It didn't take him very long to get his things ready, leaving him with the rest of the day stretched out before him and nothing to do. He wished he could read Scriptures. But the Old Books were written in an ancient and difficult language. You'd have to study hard for years, Ashrof said, before you could read them. "And the Temple would prefer you didn't read them," he would add. That was another thing that he'd explain when Jack got older.

He fretted and fidgeted through the day. Van came home a little late for supper, complaining about the councilor who had to be driven all the way out to Oziah's Wood and back the same day, just to see some cowherds who owed him money.

The hardest thing of all was getting to sleep that night; but eventually Jack managed it.

To his surprise, he didn't dream about the mountain.

Early morning found him in a little patch of woods not far from the stockade, hugging himself against the cold and grumbling against Ellayne for being late. She probably wasn't coming at all, he thought. This was a joke, a big joke on him. Or else her father had caught her out at the last minute, and Jack would be blamed for the whole thing and sold down the river to unload barges in Obann for the rest of his life. He'd get her for that.

Someone's feet crunched dead leaves and sticks.

"Oh—there you are," Ellayne said.

He hardly would have recognized her. She had boys' clothes on, stout boots on her feet, and had tucked her hair up under a floppy cloth cap that otherwise would have been too big for her.

"What kept you?" he snapped. "I'm freezing!"

"It isn't easy to sneak out of my house. The maid's very nosy. Here, I brought you some things."

She laid down her bag and from it took out a knitted wool cap and a woolen jacket decorated with a yellow check pattern. It hung loosely on Jack's shoulders, but it was the warmest garment he'd ever had on his body.

"See if these boots fit," she said. "They were my brother Josek's, but he grew out of them. The cap is Dib's, and he'll be mad when he finds out it's gone. Try not to lose it."

He had to stuff bits of torn-up cloth napkin into the toes; then the boots fit him well enough.

"I guess we're ready," he said, stomping a little to get his feet used to their new homes. "Which way is Lintum Forest?"

"It's somewhere south of here. I don't know how far. But it's a big place. It shouldn't be too hard to find."

That was good enough for Jack, because he knew no better.

CHAPTER 8

An Empty Land

Jack knew a path that wound through the little woods. Ellayne followed him.

"One thing I don't get," he said. "I'm glad you're coming with me, don't get me wrong—but why did you want to? You didn't dream about the mountain. You never thought of it until you heard me talking to Ashrof. What made you want to do this?"

She grunted as she yanked her pack free from some sticker bushes. "It's hard to explain," she said. "As soon as you said you were going to go up the mountain, I had to go, too.

"I don't know how to say it—but I want to do something! Not just grow up and marry whoever my mother and father want me to marry, and wear nice clothes, and never see anything and never know anything, except what everybody else in the world has already seen and already knows."

"Your ma and pa have been all the way to Obann lots of times," Jack said. "You'd get to see Obann."

"Anybody can do that!"

"I'm only asking because I don't want you changing your mind and wanting to go back."

"I won't!"

It didn't take long to pass through the woods. Jack noticed the green leaves were sprouting on the berry bushes just as they ought to sprout, in spite of the funny weather. Robins sang in the trees, blue jays scolded, cardinals chirped. Squirrels raced along the branches and up and down the trunks, pausing to chatter and scold.

The children emerged from the woods.

"So that's the land!" Ellayne said. "I've never seen it before. There's so much of it!"

Before them, almost as vast as the sky itself, stretched a rolling moor, wave after wave of grey-green grass and scrub and clumps of brush, with knots of trees here and there. Neither Jack nor Ellayne had ever seen the sea; few people in Obann ever had. But if you have, you will know better what the land looked like: a motionless ocean. Not a road, not a trail, not a single herd of goats or sheep or cattle with its drover, not a solitary human being on foot or on horseback—Jack had seen it before, but never really looked at it. It just went on and on until it vanished into a distant haze.

But to their left towered the mountains, lorded over by Bell Mountain itself with its crown of clouds.

"There is an awful lot of it, isn't there?" Jack said. No wonder nobody comes out here, he thought. It seemed impossible that anyone could actually cross such a space. You'd just keep walking and walking without ever getting there—wherever "there" was.

"We should keep the woods between ourselves and Ninneburky," Ellayne said, "in case anybody has started looking for us."

"Are you ready?"

"Of course I'm ready. Let's go."

They stepped off together, entering a sea of tough grey moor grass that clawed at their shins and made slishing sounds with every step. The sun by now was just peeking over the mountains. Somewhere a crow cawed.

"It does seem kind of silly not to be walking straight toward the mountains," Jack said.

"I told you—someone would catch us if we did that," Ellayne answered.

"I wonder how far it is to Lintum Forest. We can't see it from here, so it must be pretty far away."

"If we keep walking, we'll get there."

It was easier to keep walking than to keep talking. North of the river was a greener, kinder land. Any cow that tried to eat this grass, Jack thought, would be sorry. Indeed, he soon learned he'd better step over the biggest tuffets if he didn't want to be tripped up. Ellayne stubbed her toe and went down in a heap.

"Ooh! Help me up."

Jack pulled her up.

"Look," he said, pointing. She turned. "We haven't done too badly. We've left the little woods pretty far behind, and it's still between us and the town. No one will see us."

But Ellayne preferred to look ahead. "Look how empty it is, Jack," she said. "It's an awful lot of country to have nothing in it."

It was, all right, Jack thought. As far behind as they'd left the little woods, it didn't look to him like they'd made any forward progress at all.

"I wish we could fly, like birds," Ellayne said. "I'll bet the wild geese fly over this country when they fly south for the winter. I wonder how long it takes them to cross it. And I wonder where they go. *Abombalbap* says there are dragons in the south. Real ones, that breathe fire."

"We only want to go as far as Lintum Forest," Jack said. "Then we'll turn east and head for the mountains. We ought to be pretty good at long walks by then."

When the sun was high, they stopped to rest and have a bite to eat. By then they'd come far enough that they couldn't see the little woods anymore. There were too many ridges in the way. Jack and Ellayne had walked up and down those ridges.

"My legs are tired," she said.

"It's getting hot," Jack said. He took off the wool cap and put it carefully in his coat pocket and undid his buttons. There was a little breeze, and it felt good.

"I'm wondering where we ought to spend the night," Ellayne said. "Even if we had sleeping bags, I wouldn't want to sleep out here all night. It's liable to get cold. Maybe too cold."

"We'll build a fire."

"I haven't seen any rabbits yet for you to shoot at."

"There's bound to be something."

He certainly hoped there'd be something to shoot at between here and Lintum, or they'd be apt to go hungry. He took his slingshot out of his bag, picked up a few pebbles, and spent some minutes practicing. A small, rotten, broken-off tree stump made a handy target.

"Have you really killed rabbits with that?" Ellayne asked.

"Sure—and had 'em for supper. I got a woodchuck once, too."

"Well, that's something. I've never had rabbit, or woodchuck. Do they taste good?"

"By the time we get some, they'll taste great," Jack said. "Come on, we'd better get moving again. Maybe we can find a good place to stay the night."

Ellayne said, "Oh! My legs!" as she got up.

No rabbits made themselves available, but well before sundown they found a place to stay—a heap of ruins.

It was a few low, broken stone walls, some piles of jagged rubble, and a couple of broken columns that were like square stone trees. It was no kind of stone that Jack and Ellayne had ever seen before. It was as if each wall had once been a single slab of perfectly squared-off stone. Much of it was overgrown by creepers. It all sat atop a low mound that stood alone in an expanse of flat ground. The mound had steep sides, and they had a job getting to the top.

"I wonder what this was!" Jack said, turning slowly to take it all in. "Our whole town could fit on this hilltop."

"Those walls will keep us out of the wind," Ellayne said.

"I wonder if it was a town or just one great big building. It's bigger than those ruins down by the river." Jack shook his head, puzzled. "Van doesn't like ruins," he said. "He says he hears funny noises when he drives past them. But here we are, and I don't see anything."

"What does he think makes the noises?"

"He doesn't know. We'd better decide where we want to build our fire, and then pick up enough firewood before it gets dark."

This time of year they knew the cold wind came down from the mountains. They found a sturdy bit of wall between them and the east, cleared a spot for the fire, and gathered sticks and brush. Armloads of creepers torn away from their moorings would have to do for bedding.

Ellayne stuck close to Jack as they explored the hilltop. "I've never been in any ruins before," she said. "My father says there are whole ruined cities. There's a really big one right across the river from Obann."

"They're all that's left of the cities of the Empire," Jack said. "Ashrof taught me about it. It's in the Old Books, in the Prophets. A thousand years before there even was an Empire, the prophets told how God was going to destroy it. The Empire would be full of great cities, and they would all be destroyed because the people were so wicked. Only the ruins would be left, so that people would always be able to see them and never forget what God did."

"Ugh! Ashrof never taught me that," Ellayne said. "I don't know how I feel about sleeping someplace where the people were so wicked. What if there are ghosts?"

"We can't sleep out in the open. We'd freeze."

Ellayne nodded. "At that, we'd better make a big fire," she said. "At least there's plenty to burn up here. And I suppose it'll look different when the weather gets warmer and the creepers come into blossom. It won't look so dead."

CHAPTER 9

A Night in the Ruins

Even with the stone wall between them and the mountains, it was deadly cold on the hilltop once the sun went down.

Ellayne tried to start the fire by rubbing stones together to make sparks, which were supposed to ignite a little pile of dried moss she'd scraped together. "It's in Abombalbap," she said, through clenched teeth. "It's how the shepherd taught him to make fire, when he was a boy. But there's something wrong with these stones."

From his pack Jack took a little cloth bag—which he'd filled with matches. He soon had the fire going properly.

"You might've told me you had matches," Ellayne said.

"I didn't want to use them if you could start a fire with stones. As it is, Van's going to be hard put to cook his supper tonight. These are all his kitchen matches."

They built up the fire and fed it. By nightfall they had it blazing powerfully. Jack had learned from other boys how to build a campfire. Boys playing outside the stockade sometimes liked to roast potatoes.

"We really ought to learn how to make fire without matches," Ellayne said. "We won't always have matches."

"Wish we had something to cook," Jack said.

They each had an onion and some bread, shared an

apple, and washed it down with water. Tomorrow they'd have to refill their water bag somehow. There had to be a creek or a spring somewhere in this country, Jack thought.

They sat close together by the fire with their backs to the wall. The firelight glowed off another ruined wall a few yards away, and long shadows danced on it like ghosts. Somewhere else on the hilltop an owl hooted. Some tiny creature shrieked.

"What was that?"

"I suppose an owl caught a mouse," Jack said.

"I wonder if old ruins have ghosts in them," Ellayne said. "A lot of people say they do. What does the Scripture say?"

"I don't know. I haven't read the Scriptures."

"I thought Ashrof taught them to you."

"He taught me a little. Not much," Jack said. "He was going to teach me how to read the Old Books for myself, when I was older. It takes a long time to learn how to read them."

"Why didn't he just teach you from the New Books?" Ellayne said. "The books the prester and the reciters read from at meetings—that's Scripture, too, isn't it?"

Jack shook his head. "Ashrof says the New Books aren't really Scripture. They're just books about Scripture. The Old Books are very old, from before the Empire. The New Books weren't written until hundreds of years after the Empire fell."

"I don't see the difference."

"You'd have to ask Ashrof. He says God Himself told the prophets what to write in the Old Books. That's what makes them holy. The New Books aren't holy. Anyhow, that's what Ashrof says."

They went on like that for a while, mostly because neither of them liked the way the night sounded when they stopped talking. The wind went "oooh" when it blew through the ruins, and sometimes sounded like a woman weeping. It made the hilltop seem the most lonesome, forsaken place in the world. Sometimes things crunched or skittered through the underbrush in the dark. Only animals, Jack said. At least he hoped so.

"What's making that chittery-chattery-boop noise?" Ellayne said. "What kind of animal is that?"

"How should I know? I can't see it."

"It's getting on my nerves. It's as if they're all around us, watching us, and we can't see them—and they know it."

"Of course they're watching us," Jack said. "Animals are curious. There must be foxes up here and mice and other animals that come out at night. You heard the owl."

"They sound like they're awfully close."

"Don't worry so much. They won't want to come too near the fire."

Something whistled and chattered at them, and now Jack saw a pair of red lights, close to the ground, just beyond the circle of firelight. That'd be the animal's eyes, he thought. He didn't want to call Ellayne's attention to it; but in another moment she saw it, too.

"There! What's that?" she whispered.

"Quit whispering! You don't have to whisper. It's only an animal," Jack said. "You're making me jumpy, so stop it."

"I just want to know what it is."

Jack did something then to prove to himself that he wasn't getting scared. He broke off a little piece of bread and tossed it about halfway toward the red eyes. He wished he had his slingshot in his hands, but he'd put it away; and if he dug in his bag for it, he was sure the animal would run away. So instead of reaching for the slingshot, he made a clucking noise with the tip of his tongue and his front teeth. It was a noise that sometimes soothed Van's ox when it was in a bad mood.

But it was no ox that came into the light to get the bread.

Jack and Ellayne both held their breath. This was no animal whose like they'd ever seen before. Not a fox, nor a rat, nor anything they had a word for.

It came tiptoeing out on little furry feet, walking on its hind legs like a tiny human being. Indeed, it might have been a human being, if it weren't so small and covered with glossy brown fur from head to foot—except for its face, which was bare and pale and almost human.

From outside the light, the creature's eyes had shone red; but up closer they were brown, almost black, bright and shiny and large.

It tiptoed up to the bread, hesitated for a moment, and then reached down and picked it up—with hands.

Little furry hands, real hands like Jack's own: Jack didn't know what to think. All he could do was stare as the creature handled the bread with nimble fingers, studying it, sniffing it, and finally stuffing it into its mouth. Jack saw a flash of tiny white teeth.

With its cheeks bulging, the creature turned suddenly and scampered back into the darkness.

Jack and Ellayne exhaled together, loudly. Jack jumped up and only then realized he couldn't follow the creature in the dark. But he didn't sit back down. His heart raced like a moth flapping frantically when you held it by one wing.

"Tell me what that was!" Ellayne cried. "Do you know what that was? Do you?"

"Oh, shut up and let me think!"

"You don't know! But I do! I know!"

That startled him so much that he dropped down into a squat and glared at her.

"You know?" he said.

"You bet I do! Don't you know anything, Jack? That was a Skrayling, that's what it was—one of the Little People. We've seen one of the Little People. Oh, it's in all the stories! And now we have to watch ourselves because they're magic. They can put a spell on you. They can—"

He held up his hand, and Ellayne swallowed whatever she was going to say, and she stared at him. He didn't pay any attention to her. Something else, something important, was trying to batter its way through the confusion in his mind. Something Ashrof told him once, something from the Scripture. Something about the ruins.

"Just a minute!" he said. And then he had it.

"Ellayne, listen. Ashrof taught me some things about the Empire. How the ruins are all that's left of it. And he said the prophets wrote all about it before any of it ever happened. And he recited a verse about the ruins. It went like this, or something like it: *And none shall dwell there forever, but only the Omah shall possess those cities, and shall dance therein.*

"I asked him who the Omah was, and he said it was an old word that nobody uses anymore. No one's sure what it means, but he said most of the scholars who study those things say Omah means 'the hairy ones.' Well, what we just saw was hairy enough."

"Hairy ones?" Ellayne repeated.

"It's in the Old Books," Jack said. "The Empire was going to build a hundred great cities, and God was going to destroy them and give them to the Omah."

"But are they good or bad?" Ellayne said.

"I don't know! Ashrof didn't say."

"Well, he should've! What are those things going to do to us if we fall asleep up here?"

"I don't know that either," Jack said. "But I'm thinking we'd better not fall asleep. I don't think I could sleep now anyhow. Could you?"

She shook her head.

"It didn't look like a bad kind of creature," he added.

"That was only one," Ellayne said. "What if there are hundreds of them up here—and they come out and swarm all over us?"

Jack built up the fire. Fortunately they'd collected more than enough wood; they wouldn't run out.

"I just wish we could've gotten a better look at it," he said.

"Any kind of look is bad luck," Ellayne said, shivering in her coat. "I think those Omah and the Little People are the same thing. They don't like to be seen. They can put an enchantment on you. They can turn you into stone, or else turn you into their slave, and you can't get away—never. They take you underground and keep you there forever, and you never get any older. There was one man that they let out, and as soon as the sun came up, he crumbled into dust."

Jack could have done without that story. "Well, I don't see why the one we saw should want to do anything bad to us. I gave it some bread, didn't I?"

As their excitement ebbed at last, and as the fire toasted them, they found themselves so weary that they couldn't have stayed awake no matter how badly they thought they had to. The full day of tramping over the wild plain took its toll.

The next thing Jack knew, the sun was up, birds were singing in the underbrush, and Ellayne slept against him with her head pillowed on his shoulder.

We're still alive, he thought. He wondered if the night's adventure had been a dream. It certainly seemed like one, by light of day. And he was hungry and thirsty—

That was when he noticed the rabbit laid out at his feet.

And squatting by the ashes of the campfire, the little hairy man.

CHAPTER 10

The Hairy Ones Dance

When it saw Jack's eyes were open, it made a soft whistling noise at him. Jack found he wasn't in the least afraid of it, not now. The only way a fresh-killed rabbit came to rest in front of him was if someone had put it there as a gift. And there was no someone besides this little manlike creature.

Jack clicked his tongue. The animal's round head bobbed up and down, and it chattered back at him.

The noise woke Ellayne, and when she saw what was making it, she shrank up against Jack with a loud gasp.

"It's all right," he said. "It's friendly. Look—it brought us a rabbit. That's because I gave it bread last night. This meat's going to taste mighty good."

Ellayne stared at the Omah (if that's what it was). The Omah looked up at her and made a purring noise, almost like a cat.

"How long has he been here?"

"He was here when I woke up," Jack said.

"Give him another piece of bread. Maybe he'll go away."

Jack reached into his bag. The visitor watched intently, but didn't startle or run away. Jack broke off a piece of bread and held it out at arm's length.

"Here, fellow—nice bread. Come and get it."

Bold as you please, the creature stood up on its hind legs, walked up to Jack, and took the bread from him. By light of day you could see its hands really were hands and not just paws. Aside from being furry, they were perfect miniature hands.

It stood right there by Jack and ate the bread, showing no fear at all. Jack had known squirrels that would eat from your fingers, but they were always fidgety about it.

This little creature wasn't.

"It really is friendly," Ellayne said. "It certainly likes our bread."

"Good boy," Jack said.

The animal (if it was an animal) swallowed the last of the bread and began to chirp, chatter, twitter, and whistle at them, repeatedly pointing to the rabbit.

"Burn me if he isn't talking to us—or trying to!" Ellayne said. "He wants us to eat the rabbit. I'm sure that's what he's saying. Oh, Jack, I am hungry!"

Jack had brought along Van's best knife for just this purpose; and having done it before, he soon had the rabbit skinned and cleaned. Their new friend snatched up the rabbit skin and ran off into the brush with it.

"What does your book say about that?" Jack said.

"There's nothing like this in the book," Ellayne said. "It's funny—now that I've seen him up close, I hope he comes back."

They made a fire, and Jack did his best with the rabbit. He'd never cooked one outdoors before over a campfire. He would have done much better in a kitchen, but they were too hungry to complain about the raw spots or the burned spots. They ate the whole thing and licked the juice from their fingers.

"Now we'd better try to find some water," Jack said. "The skin's almost empty."

They commenced to explore the hilltop. Now that they had more time, and reasonably full bellies, they discovered that the entire hilltop was a single mass of ruins, much grown over with brush and creepers, with here and there a stunted tree. Jack was sure there must be water somewhere; otherwise the plants wouldn't grow.

"I wonder if it's a real hill at all," Ellayne said, "or just one gigantic ruin. My father says they built the wall around the city of Obann with stones taken from the ancient wall, and there's still plenty of the ancient wall left over. I wonder why people can't build so big anymore."

They were standing in the middle of a broad, flat, tussocky area, with a few bare spots that showed that there was a stone floor underneath it all, when they heard a chirp and a chatter. As if by magic the Omah appeared in front of them, popping out from behind a bush. He might have been following them all along, and they never knowing he was near.

"Hello, there!" Ellayne said. "I wish you could tell us your name. You wouldn't happen to know where we might find water, would you?"

The Omah turned and took a few steps, stopped and looked over its shoulder at them, and chirped.

"He wants us to follow him," Ellayne said. "I think he understood me."

"Maybe that's the magic," Jack said. "Come on."

It was just like following a dog or a cat that wanted to

be fed and was showing you the way to its dish. Every few steps, the creature stopped to chirp at them.

It led them to a big evergreen shrub, behind which was a high pile of compacted dirt and a black hole in the ground. There were stone steps leading down into the hole. Ellayne stopped short.

"He wants to take us underground. That's in the stories!" she said.

"I'll go. You stay up here," Jack said. "But I'll bet there's water down there."

"What—stay up here alone?"

"I'm going. Maybe there's treasure down there, too."

The Omah hopped down one step and paused to chatter loudly at them. Jack followed. "You'll never come back!" Ellayne said. But he'd never heard the stories that her father used to read to her from books, and saw no harm in following the Omah down the stairs.

It was cool and dark in the stairwell, and who could say how many centuries it had been since anyone had ventured down that way? But almost as soon as he started, Jack smelled water. And it wasn't such a long way. From the bottom of the stairs, and the hard stone floor that waited there, he could look up and see the top, and Ellayne's anxious face framed in the opening.

"It's all right," he called up to her.

"Be careful!"

The Omah whistled. Jack turned, and a few steps away, he saw a regular lake of dark, cold water stretching into the shadows as far as his eye could see. The stone ceiling above it rested on huge stone columns.

But this was a lake with a perfectly straight stone shore:

as if men with unimaginable powers had carved it out of the bedrock of the earth.

"Ellayne! Water!" Jack's call set off an avalanche of echoes. Had he known a little more about caverns and other such places under the earth, he might not have been so loud.

He knelt by the stone shoreline, wetted his fingertips, and tasted the water. He cupped his hands and tried a mouthful. It was cold and sweet, nothing wrong with it at all—not like rain water that had sat in a barrel for some time.

Jack drank until he was full, then filled the water bag and went back up the stairs. The Omah darted ahead of him and came up first.

"See?" Jack said. "Nothing bad happened. And I've got water, plenty of it. Here, have some. It's good."

Ellayne drank her fill from the waterskin. By and by, they walked to the edge of the hilltop and looked out on the plain. The Omah accompanied them, not bothering anymore to hide.

Jack had hoped to see some sign of Lintum Forest in the south, but even from the top of the hill, you couldn't see that far. They could see nothing but an endless, dreary expanse of grey plain with a few isolated hills in the distance—hills that were probably ruins like this one.

"It doesn't seem right that such a big country should be so empty," Ellayne said.

"You said something like that yesterday," Jack said. "Well, yes, it does look like something's wrong with it. There ought to be life on it, but it looks dead."

"I wonder if it always was," Ellayne said.

They decided to spend another night on the hilltop, resting. Once they came down, they'd have a long, hard way to go. Maybe Jack could shoot a rabbit or two to take with them.

"And I'd like for you to cut off my hair, before the knife gets dull, so I can pass as a boy," Ellayne said. "Someday we're bound to meet people, and some of them might be bad. Better if they think I'm a boy. Besides, if my father sends out the militia, they'll be looking for a boy and a girl, not two boys."

They returned to their campsite. Jack gave the Omah another piece of bread while Ellayne let down her hair and combed it free of snarls. The Omah watched with interest.

"Ready?" Jack asked.

"Go ahead."

Jack cut Van's hair and Van cut his; but they used scissors and Van's razor. Cutting a girl's hair with a knife was a different story altogether. He took his time and did his best to make it look not too horrible.

As he cut off lengths of her hair and tossed them aside, the Omah scampered back and forth excitedly, gathering up the hair as it fell. Ellayne laughed at his antics.

"He really likes my hair," she said. "I wonder what he's going to do with it."

"It'd make a nice lining for his nest, I guess," Jack said.

When he'd finished, he was glad they hadn't brought along a mirror. A barber needed scissors, not a knife.

The Omah collected all the hair and ran off.

"I look terrible now, don't I?" Ellayne said.

"Hair grows back," Jack said. "I'm sorry it looks so bad. I should've thought to bring scissors."

"At least I don't have to look at it."

They settled down to have an apple, basking in the noonday sun. Now that he knew it had a plentiful supply of water, Jack wondered why people didn't live on the hilltop. With a stockade and a watchtower, it'd be safe from enemies. They could run herds on the plain and probably grow crops.

But God gave the ruins to the hairy ones, the Old Books said. People avoided ruins. He wished he could ask Ashrof about it. He wished he could read the Scriptures for himself.

An outburst of loud whistling and screeching shattered the peace.

"Now what!" Ellayne cried.

Jack got up, but couldn't see anything. The racket was deafening.

"It's the Omahs—sounds like a hundred of 'em," he said. "There must be hundreds of them living up here. Something's got them all stirred up."

Just as suddenly as it started, the noise broke off. Jack went out to the bare spot, expecting to see a mob of little men. Ellayne followed, warning him to be careful. He wouldn't have been surprised to find dozens of dead Omahs lying about: it sounded as if they might have had a riot.

But there was nothing.

"Where are they?" Jack said.

"We don't know anything about them." Ellayne stood close enough to clutch Jack's arm. "We don't know whether they're animals or people, or neither, or both. There's no telling what they might do."

"I hope ours is all right," Jack said. He whistled, softly at first, then louder. After a few moments, some high-pitched whistles answered him.

Out from behind a screen of creepers came ten of the little hairy ones. Ellayne jumped. Jack felt his muscles tighten.

"They're smiling!" Ellayne said.

To Jack they all looked alike, and they were all smiling, showing bright white teeth. He noticed that their eyeteeth were longer and sharper than the others. A bite from an Omah might be nasty. Bites from ten of them might be a lot worse than nasty. But even their teeth weren't the most noticeable thing about them.

Each of them clutched a handful of Ellayne's hair and waved it vigorously, like children playing with pinwheels.

"They look happy," Jack said.

They started chattering again, and before you knew it, they'd formed a line and were parading in a circle around the two children, hopping, chirping, and brandishing the golden hair.

"Are they dancing?" Ellayne said. "I really think they're dancing!"

"Just don't move," Jack said.

The Omahs danced around them several times, and then all darted off at once in different directions, vanishing like smoke into the underbrush.

CHAPTER 11

Manawyttan

While the little hairy men were dancing around Ellayne, waving locks of her hair, Ellayne's father, the chief councilor, was trying not to dance. But he was so angry that he found it hard to keep his feet on the floor.

Roshay Bault had not seen his daughter since he'd kissed her good night the night before. A whole day had gone by, and a whole night, and half of another day. And because he was an intelligent man, as Ellayne said, he wound up at the chamber house demanding answers from the prester. The prester had Ashrof brought in so that he could demand answers from him; and they soon worked it out that Ellayne had gone off to climb Bell Mountain, in company with the half-witted stepson of a municipal carter. Van was sent for, too. The chief councilor had more than enough wrath to pour out on them all.

"I'll send men on horseback up the river after them," the chief said, "and a fast rider to Obann with a letter to the Temple demanding the immediate installation of a new prester who is not an idiot. You had all better pray that my daughter is back under my roof by this time tomorrow!"

"My dear sir," said the prester, "I understand how you feel. But how far can a couple of children get on foot? Your men are sure to overtake them—have no doubt of it. But surely it's unjust to say the chamber house bears any blame.

"Really, it's all the boy's fault. Who knows what he told Ellayne to get her to go with him? Children sometimes have fantastic notions. But you have heard from the reciter how he tried to dissuade the boy from his insane idea. How could he have known your daughter was involved? Neither of the children ever mentioned it."

"Excuses! Lily-livered excuses! I'm not interested!" the chief thundered. "I sent my daughter here to learn her letters, not to be lured into a suicidal prank. The boy told the teacher what he was going to do, and the old fool didn't stop him. And neither did the stepfather!"

Van quaked and stammered.

"But sir, I know nothing, not a thing!" he said. "Jack isn't even my son. He was always mooning about, ever since his mother died. I've never understood him. He never tells me what he's thinking. He is not quite right in the head. If only this fool of a teacher had told me, I would have put a stop to this. I swear!"

Ellayne's father glared at them all. He was not chief councilor for nothing, and they knew it.

"I'll be burned," he said, "if I don't see the lot of you as beggars in rags before this is over."

Ellayne was not thinking of her father.

Hours before sundown, the Omahs brought them two more rabbits for their supper, and a thing that Jack said was a baby woodchuck, and a heap of greens with white swellings below—wild onions, with a nice wild smell. All the Omahs that they saw had made themselves armlets or necklaces of Ellayne's hair.

"We'll save the rabbits for tomorrow," Jack said. "This woodchuck'll be plenty for tonight."

"You'd better give them all some bread," Ellayne said.

They had a grand supper, all they wanted to eat and drink, and a grand fire to keep off the chill. The Omahs seemed to enjoy watching them build the fire, clean and cook the woodchuck. Jack gutted the rabbits and wrapped them in the woodchuck's hide.

When night fell, and their bellies were full, and the fire crackled busily, Ellayne told Jack one of the stories from her book. Several Omahs squatted by the fire. She was sure that they were listening to the story.

"When Abombalbap first rode out on adventures," she said, "he got lost in Lintum Forest, and he might have died before he found the way out again. But the Seven Hags of Balamadda rescued him just before he starved to death, and brought him back to their secret place in the middle of the forest. They used magic so that all the paths would bend away from it and no one would find the place unless they knew stronger magic.

"They nursed him back to health, and told him they read it in the stars that he was born to be a hero, and someday he would heal the Wounded King of the Dolorous Marches, and all that land would be green again. So they gave him a sword and a spear, a shield and armor, and taught him how to be a warrior. They knew more about that than anybody else. And after they'd taught him, Abombalbap could drive his spear right through the trunk of a tree and cut a man in half from crown to crotch with his sword.

"But the evil witch, Raddamallicom, found out about it all, and she plotted to lure Abombalbap into her castle and trick him into drinking a poison potion. The Little People in the forest, the Skraylings, were her slaves, and they spied on the Seven Hags and told her everything. She made a plan to make Abombalbap believe the hags were only pretending to be good to him and that they were going to kill him and make a magic potion from his heart's blood that would make them all young and beautiful again. It wasn't true, but Abombalbap didn't know—"

Somewhere down below, out on the desolate plain, rose up a howl that stopped Ellayne's story.

It was a long, lamenting howl that started low and climbed higher and higher until it was a marrow-chilling shriek, like a giant claw scraping on ice. Ellayne clapped her hands over her ears and tried to scream, but Jack clapped a hand over her mouth and held it there.

And then the shrieking stopped.

The Omahs stood up and chattered quietly.

"I didn't want it to hear you," Jack said, "—whatever it was." He took his hand away, and Ellayne took a deep breath.

"God defend us!" she said (that was how the prester ended the Great Prayer that everyone in town prayed together, once a year). "Do you suppose it saw our fire? What if it was wolves? Wolves kill people!"

"I don't think wolves would want to come too close to a fire. And I don't think our little friends would live up here if wolves came up. See—they're not afraid. That's a good sign."

She was relieved that the Omahs hadn't run away, that they were slowly sitting back down.

"Oh, Jack! I wish we could talk to them, and they to us.

They'd tell us what it was that made that horrible noise."

"The country's not so empty as it looks," Jack said. "Maybe it's not good for us to stay in any one place for too long. I'll be glad to be moving on tomorrow. There's a long way to go to the mountain."

"I wish we had swords and spears and armor," Ellayne said.

"And seven hags to teach us how to use them! What happened, Ellayne? I want to know! I never heard a story like that. The only stories I know are a few from the Scriptures that Ashrof taught me. He kept promising to teach me more, when I was older." Jack grinned. "Ha! I guess we'll have a story of our own before we're done."

The horrible howl was not repeated. Ellayne tried, but she couldn't pick up the thread of her story. Nestled together against the cold, the children fell asleep at last. The last thing Jack remembered thinking, before he dropped off, was what a host of stars shone over them and that God, who put them in the sky, knew the names of each and every one of them.

They woke early, chilled and stiff, and got busy right away to warm themselves. They repacked their bags, refilled the waterskin, ate a breakfast of bread and cheese, and made sure they knew which way was south before they climbed down to the plain. It was a clear day with the mountains rising in the east, looking close enough to reach out and touch.

Getting down the weathered, gully-stricken slope of the hill, without taking a hard fall, occupied their full attention. Stickers clutched at them on every side. The sun was well above the mountains by the time they stood on level ground again.

"Well, that's that," Jack said. "Let's see if we can make the next hilltop before sundown. If they're all ruins, maybe they'll all have water, and walls to protect us from the wind."

"The next hill looks mighty far away," Ellayne said.

Something chirped, making them jump. Up from a grey tussock, practically at Jack's feet, sprang an Omah. It carried a sharpened stick like a spear and wore Ellayne's hair around its neck.

"Look who's here!" Jack said. Ellayne beamed. "I think he wants to come with us," she said. "I'm sure he does!"

"Let's find out."

They set off, and the little furry man scampered along with them, chittering merrily, finding his way effortlessly around the tussocks.

"Fellow, we're very glad to have you," Jack said.

"Jack, you can't just call him 'Fellow.' It's impolite. We have to give him a name."

"Maybe by the time we think of one, he'll have left us," Jack said.

But the Omah stayed with them all day, and Ellayne decided to call him Manawyttan, after a hero in one of her old tales.

"The name's bigger than he is," Jack said. "Let's just call him Wytt."

CHAPTER 12

A Camp in a Cave

They made good progress that day. Sometimes Wytt disappeared, but never for long. Under a low bush coming into purple bloom, he showed them a nest with eggs in it, pale green with dark green speckles. Jack put them carefully into his pack. Wytt broke into one with his sharp stick and sucked out the contents.

"I hope we don't have to eat them like that," Ellayne said.

"I'll boil them if we have enough water," Jack answered.

The next hilltop drew them on, and by pushing hard, they got there late in the afternoon. But they didn't go up to the top. At the foot of a deep gully about halfway up the slope, where they would have missed it in the shadows, Wytt showed them a hole that turned out to be a man-made cave in the side of the hill, with a flat stone floor and a curved roof of tightly fitted bricks.

"Do you think we should stop here for the night?" Jack said. The Omah whistled and bobbed his head.

"I think he understands every word we say," Ellayne said. "If only we could understand him! We probably don't have time to get up to the top and set up camp before dark. I suppose it's best we stop here. But I don't like being underground."

They had to prepare their fire right away, while they still had light. The slope was overgrown with brush, with some big pieces here and there that had fallen off trees. Jack used two more of his matches to get the fire going, and wondered how much longer they'd last. Maybe they'd come to a town where they could buy some more—if things like matches were for sale out here, far from the great river that carried most of Obann's commerce.

Night fell before they'd finished their supper. The rabbits were splendid, and the eggs would serve for breakfast. While they were still eating, Wytt went off somewhere.

"Probably having a look-round," Jack said. "I think he can see in the dark. If there are Omahs on this hill, he'll want to find out about them."

"Do you think the Omahs on different hilltops know each other?" Ellayne said. "Maybe they go on visits from one hill to the next."

Jack made a torch. "To see how far back this cave goes," he explained, "and what else is in it."

"Hadn't that better wait till daylight? What if it's dangerous?"

"It'll be just as dark back there by day as by night. And I'm not sleepy."

Ellayne didn't want to be left behind; and as they were already in the cave, going farther in wouldn't be that much worse, she thought. She made a torch, too, and they went together.

"Watch out for holes in the floor," she said.

Nothing like this had ever been built in Ninneburky. The front of Ellayne's house was brick, but not like this. These bricks were as smooth as glass to the touch, and they fit together perfectly. A tall man on tiptoe couldn't have touched the curved ceiling of the passage.

"Look at this floor," Jack said. "It's all one sheet of stone and as flat as a slate. It's like they melted the rock and poured it out. How did they do things like that?"

"And rusty somethings stuck in the ceiling," Ellayne said, holding her torch over her head and looking up. "What was this place?"

"Who knows? Something they built in Empire days."

How far they went, they couldn't have said. It was all the same: a straight passage into the side of the ruin, unvarying in its level floor and glassy brick. Their shadows capered along the walls, distorted by wavering torchlight. The children plodded on and on, and began to wonder if the passage would take them clear to the opposite side of the hill. But it didn't.

Jack stepped on something that crunched under his boot. That stopped them. Until then, the floor had been as clean as if someone swept it every day.

He moved his foot and looked down.

"All over the floor!" he said. "I think it's bones."

Ellayne choked back a cry and clutched his arm. She didn't speak, but pointed ahead with her torch.

Jack caught his breath.

Just ahead of them, bones choked the passage almost to the ceiling. It was as if someone had dumped them by the cartload—many cartloads. They lay in heaps. And many of them were skulls, round and white with black eye sockets, broken teeth, and fleshless jaws gaping. Out of the midst of the bone pile rose an iron staircase with a rusted handrail.

"This is as far as we go," Jack said. Ellayne nodded, not

daring to speak. They backed away together until darkness swallowed the bones, then turned and hurried back to their fire.

The fire had almost burned out while they were gone, and it took some doing to build it back up without using up another precious match. Not that they needed the warmth, Ellayne thought. She was sweating like mad, but without feeling at all overheated. She saw it dripping off Jack's forehead, too. But to do without a blazing fire just now would be unthinkable.

"I don't know how we can sleep here tonight," she said.

"We have to sleep here. There's nowhere else," Jack said. "Think I like sleeping by all those dead men's bones? But I'll bet there were plenty of dead people on the other hilltop, and it was all right. We just didn't see them."

"Well, I wish we could say prayers. It's too bad we don't have a prester."

"Ashrof says you don't need a prester. You just say a prayer, and God hears it."

That almost made Ellayne forget the bones. "He said that? But how can you pray when you're not in the chamber house and you don't have the prester to lead you?"

"He did say the prester wouldn't like it if he heard him saying that," Jack said. "But Ashrof says that's how it is in the Old Books. When people in Old Obann wanted to say a prayer, they just said one. I guess we could, too."

Ellayne thought about the bones, shivered, and said, "Yes, let's! We can pretend we're in chamber."

They took off their hats and stood together. Not having a prester to say a prayer that they could repeat after him, they couldn't help feeling they were doing something improper. But what was proper in a cave full of dead men's bones?

"God, please watch over us and keep us safe tonight—and help us get to the mountain," was all Jack could do. Ellayne prayed, "And don't be angry with us for not having a prester." And they both said, "So be it," which was how the prester always finished a prayer in chamber.

It did make them feel better. They sat down by the fire and looked out the entrance of the cave at the stars above, at the plain below. A hard day's hiking, a good supper, a few moments of intense excitement, a cozy fire, and a prayer—that was enough to send them to sleep much sooner than they would have expected.

Jack woke up wide awake with the grey morning in his eyes and the song of Bell Mountain ringing in his mind.

He'd had the dream again, clearer than ever. His whole body tingled. The fear that always gripped him when the mountain sang released its hold as soon as he opened his eyes, leaving him with a fierce desire to see the mountain. He got up, stiff and sore, but too excited to notice.

Ellayne slept on. He did notice Wytt was back, curled up beside her like a pet cat.

Never mind—he wanted to see the mountain.

With his breath making white puffs in the predawn chill, Jack scrambled up to the top of the hill, bulling his way through barricades of wiry underbrush, sometimes crawling on his hands and knees, racing up the slope. He came out on top and turned to the east.

Silent now, Bell Mountain towered proudly over the others with its crown of clouds taking on a tint of gold as the sun rose beyond the wall of peaks. Jack stretched and took deep breaths. The cold air was like a drink of water to a thirsty plowman.

Ashrof was right, he thought: you didn't need a prester. God heard those prayers we said last night, he thought. Heard them and wasn't angry, and sent him his dream again to prove it. He knew the mountain was far away, a march of many, many days—but there it was. And he was going to climb it.

"Thank you, God," he said.

He turned to face south, to get a first look at the ground they'd have to cover that day. The grey plain rolled on below him with other isolated hilltops visible. And something else—

A shadow, a dark shadow, just barely visible, due south.

Lintum Forest.

CHAPTER 13

The Theologian and the Assassin

There is not much to tell of that day's journey. As hard as they pressed to reach the next hilltop, it was too far away, and they had to spend the night on the plain.

It was not as bad as they'd feared. Wytt led them to a place where a trickle of clean, cold water welled out of a crack in the earth to become a little pool. Trees grew all around it, providing some shelter from the wind. Once Jack had the fire going, and they'd piled up dead leaves, dead reeds, as much as they could gather, to make their beds, "It won't be so bad," Ellayne said. They slept under the stars, and aside from a little extra shivering and stiffness the next morning, they were well able to continue their trek.

They would have been astounded to know that as they stopped, hours later, for rest and a bite to eat, their names were on the lips of a very important personage.

Far away in Obann City, in the Temple itself, in a very nicely appointed private study with thick rugs and rich hangings on the walls, the First Prester, Lord Reesh, angrily rattled a sheet of reed paper in his hand.

"Do you know what this is?" he said. "It's a letter from the burned fool who's the prester at the new chamber house in a place called Ninneburky. It's almost all the way up the river."

"I know the town, my lord," said the other man in the room—an unremarkable-looking fellow with a sad face and a little pointed beard.

"Good. Because you're going there," Lord Reesh said. "As soon as I explain this.

"Two children from Ninneburky have run away to climb Bell Mountain. You are to find them. If they are still on their way to the mountain when you overtake them, don't interfere. Follow them. See to it that they get there. I want to know every single thing that happens to them, Martis. If they climb the mountain, climb after them. If they get to the top and find a bell, you are to prevent them from touching it, and no one is ever to see or hear from them again."

The people of Ninneburky, even the prester himself, would have been appalled to learn that the First Prester had a confidential servant whose duties included killing people. For that is what Martis did, in addition to ferreting out secrets, spying, stealing, and arranging for certain persons to be accused of and punished for crimes they hadn't committed. Not even the other oligarchs knew about Martis. To everyone in the city, he was only a clerk in the Temple. He even looked like a clerk.

But to Lord Reesh—who considered himself the first oligarch as well as the First Prester—he was a very necessary tool. And because he had served Lord Reesh for years, and never failed him, Martis enjoyed a certain liberty in speaking to his master.

"Do you think a pair of children might actually climb the mountain, my lord?" he said.

Reesh snorted, and dropped himself into the sturdy, well-padded chair behind his hardwood desk. He was old and fat, and the letter had jangled his nerves.

"Don't tell me you haven't made a study of the Scriptures, Martis," he said.

"I am aware of the verse in Penda in which King Ozias speaks his intention to place a bell atop Mount Yul, sir. It's not recorded whether he actually did so. I'm surprised Your Lordship takes it seriously."

"I know the verse, and you know the verse," Reesh said, "but there's no way under the sun that an ignorant boy in an upriver village knows the verse! But then he didn't get his idea from studying the Old Books. According to the prester in Ninneburky—who's too scared out of his skin to lie—the curs't boy dreamed it. He dreamed about the bell on Bell Mountain!"

"Surely someone at the chamber house put the notion in his head," Martis said.

"Don't be so reasonable, Martis. It irritates me. I'm the theologian here, not you. And I say that if a child has a dream like this, there's a fair chance that he'll get to the top of the mountain. Besides which—I've had the same dream myself."

To this Martis had no answer, and was wise enough not to venture a foolish one.

"I'm an old man," Reesh went on, "and I've seen and heard many things. Of course there have always been lunatics who tried to climb Bell Mountain. Most of them died trying. A few, madder than the rest, pretended they'd been to the top and come back down. My predecessors in this office silenced them.

"Even if I were convinced that these two children were as deluded as the others, now is hardly the time to indulge such fantasy. By this time next year, we shall have a major war on our hands, and we won't want the people distracted by talk of Bell Mountain. But in this case, Martis, it's not just idle talk and moonshine. The boy's dream proves it."

"My lord, that is an extraordinary thing for you to say."

"Do you think it gives me pleasure to say it? I, who've believed in nothing all my life but the stability of the state and the mission of the Temple to hold the state together while we all try to claw our way out of barbarism?

"Until I received this letter, I dismissed my own dreams as the ramblings of an overworked mind in its old age. Now I suppose that if we made an investigation, we'd find that many people have had this dream—the very old, the very young; slaves and shepherds and servant girls; trappers alone in the woods. You know what I mean."

Martis nodded. He knew. "There is a verse in Prophet Ika, I believe," he said, "about such people having dreams."

Lord Reesh glared at his servant, as if to pierce him with his pale blue eyes—tired and old and watery, but for a moment keen as steel.

"If there is a bell up on that mountain, Martis, I want to know," he said. "And under no circumstances is that bell to be rung. If it is ever to be rung, that decision will be made here, in this office, by me or by my successor."

Martis bowed. "I understand perfectly, my lord. You can rely on me."

Lord Reesh was glad Martis hadn't made a fuss about assassinating children.

This was the day Jack made his first kill with the slingshot. It was a lucky shot, right in the head.

"Jack, you got him! Our supper!" Ellayne cried. But Jack was already on the run, in case his prey was only stunned and were to get up and run away before he could lay his hands on it.

Jack had not shot a rabbit or a woodchuck, but a good-sized bird that ran about in zigzags instead of trying to fly away. It had long legs and a long neck, and it was like no bird Jack had ever seen or heard of. Its feathers were colored a dirty white with brown streaks and speckles. It had big orange eyes and a sturdy hooked bill that was more like a hawk's bill than anything else—if there could be such a thing as a long-legged hawk that ran instead of flew. Certainly its wings looked like the bird ought to have been able to fly, if it wanted to. And it had a crest of long black feathers at the back of its head.

Jack's lucky shot had killed it outright, and there it lay.

"What kind of bird is that?" Ellayne wondered.

"I don't know. It looks like something that might be in that book of yours."

"Do you think it's fit for eating?"

"We're going to find out by eating it," Jack said. "It's big enough to make a good supper."

Wytt summoned them with a burst of chirps and whistles. He'd found the bird's nest. It was just a hole in the ground, lined with soft feathers, and the large grey eggs looked like stones. Ellayne took all four of them for their breakfast.

They'd come far enough the day before to gain the next hilltop with time to spare. Like the first, its flattened top was a scattering of ruins, isolated bits of wall and cracked pavement. But what most interested them was the view from the top, facing south.

"So that's Lintum Forest!" Ellayne said. "We ought to be there in another day or two. But please—no going in! It stretches for as far as the eye can see. If we ever got lost in there, we'd never find our way out."

"It can't be so bad, if King Ozias was born there," Jack said.

"My father says it's full of outlaws and rebels. And witches, too, I expect."

"It is part of Obann, though. There must be settlers and foresters."

"Only a fool would go in."

They made camp under the shelter of a sturdy wall, had the bird for supper (rabbit was a lot tastier, Jack thought), and fell asleep by their fire. Wytt found water in the morning, and once they'd refilled their waterskin, they set off toward the forest.

Martis, having made excellent time on horseback by traveling straight through the night along the River Road, was already halfway to Ninneburky.

CHAPTER 14

Hesket the Tinker

You could see the forest from the hilltop, but not from the plain. But knowing it was there made a difference. Ellayne didn't think her legs were half as tired as they were yesterday. Funny, she thought, the forest had been there all along. Never having seen it, still they'd believed it was there; and so believing, they'd made a great march south across the empty plain. It made her think that King Ozias' bell was really there, too, waiting for them atop the mountain.

"I think the grass is getting greener," Jack said, after they'd hiked a long way without saying anything.

"I do believe it is," Ellayne said. "And look—there are little yellow flowers in it."

They went a little farther, devoting all their energies to the march, until an unexpected sound startled them—the clank of metal on metal.

A man appeared before them, with a donkey in tow, as startling a sight as could be imagined on that uninhabited plain. He must have come up from lower ground because they didn't see him until he topped a rise right in front of them. He carried a staff and wore a broad-brimmed hat, and his donkey carried a massive pack that included some pots and pans that clanked against each other.

Jack and Ellayne stopped in their tracks. Wytt disappeared into the grass and underbrush. The man saw them just as he started down from the top of the rise, but he didn't stop. He did grin at them.

"Well, well!" he said. "Who would've thought to run into any company out here? Hello there, my pups! What brings you out here to the middle of nowhere?"

Jack didn't like being called a pup, and he didn't know what to say. All he could think was that somehow this man would try to take them back to Ninneburky. He wondered if they ought to try to run away. The man was short and stout with short legs. He might not be able to catch them.

Before he could make up his mind, Ellayne answered for them.

"We're on our way to Lintum Forest," she said, "to visit the Seven Hags of Balamadda. Can you tell us how much farther it is?"

"Aye, that I can," said the man. "But if we're going to swap yarns and enjoy each other's company, why don't we settle down and have a fire? I'll brew us some tea.

"Hesket the Tinker, that's my name. This land is my land, as I'm the only one who makes use of it. Who might you be, and where do you come from? It's been a long, long time since I've met anyone out here."

"I'm Tom, and this is my brother, Jack," Ellayne said. "We come from Obann City, and we've come a long way."

Hesket whistled in his beard—black, shot through with grey. "Indeed you have!" he said. "Obann City, is it? Never been there myself. Always meant to go someday, but who knows if that day will ever come? But why are we standing here? Pick up some sticks, and let's have a fire."

Jack didn't like him, but could hardly say so to his face. What did Ellayne have to go telling tales for? And there she was, already gathering fuel for a fire. All he could do was go along with it.

So they had a fire, and Hesket pulled a pot from the donkey's pack and a couple of tin cups, and they had tea—when they should have been pressing on to the forest, Jack thought.

"What are you doing out here, Mr. Hesket?" Ellayne asked. "We've been walking on this plain for days and days, and haven't seen a soul."

"Oh, I wander about. That's my nature," Hesket said. "But I'm surprised that two lads like you should've come so far. And who are these seven hags? I never heard of them."

"Well, they're quite famous," Ellayne said, as Jack marveled at her. "Everyone's heard of them in Obann."

"It seems to me I ought to go along with you, just to make sure you get there safe and sound," Hesket said. "There are a lot of queer people where you're headed."

"But then you'd have to turn around," Ellayne said. "There's no need for you to go out of your way. We'll be all right."

"To me, one way's as good as another. So it's settled: I'm going with you. Here, now, have some more tea. Your brother Jack don't talk much, do he?"

Hesket filled their cups again. Burn him, Jack thought. Ordinarily he liked a cup of tea when he could get it, and to be fair, Hesket's tea was as good as any Jack had ever tasted. But they were wasting time; and besides which, he felt funny. He felt a great deal more tired than he had any right to be. It was an odd kind of tired, almost as if his legs were trying to go to sleep on him.

"Jack can't talk much," Ellayne said. "That's why we're going to see the hags. They'll know how to heal him and make him just as quick in his wits as anybody else."

"They must be a remarkable bunch of hags," Hesket said.

Jack's head swam. He wanted to stand up and say they really had to be on their way; but when he tried, his legs buckled. He was asleep before he hit the ground, and never felt it.

Cold woke him—that, and someone tugging fitfully at his wrists.

He opened his eyes and saw stars. Night! How could it be?

Wytt chittered at him. Then he saw that the Omah was standing on his belly, jerking and chewing at a scratchy rope that bound his wrists.

Ellayne lay next to him, asleep on her back, wrists and ankles tied. For just another moment, Jack was confused. Then understanding came to him with a jolt, and he almost sat up—which would have bucked Wytt off him just as he was trying to set him free.

"Hurry, Wytt!"

The little man chattered loudly, like an angry squirrel. Clearly he was doing the best he could, as fast as he could, and didn't want any scolding. Jack waited, and silently wished the Omah wouldn't make any more noise. Wherever Hesket was, Jack wanted to be free before he came back.

A few more minutes passed, and Wytt broke through the rope around Jack's wrists. Jack sat up to untie his ankles.

Only then did he see Hesket lying on his back a few paces away.

The fire was out. At first Jack thought the man was sleeping. But sleeping men breathe, and Hesket wasn't breathing. His mouth gaped open. He was dead.

The moon and the stars gave light enough for Jack to see dark blood dried all over the man's face, and Wytt's sharp stick protruding from Hesket's left eye. It had been driven in deep enough to kill. The man's dead hands clutched mittfuls of grass, and one of his knees stuck up.

Panting, Jack fumbled at his ankles until he got them free. Stiff and sore, he rolled onto his hands and knees. Nearby, the hobbled donkey watched with only mild interest.

Who killed the man? There could be only one answer.

"Wytt!" he cried. "I don't know how you did it, but you've saved us. Good boy!"

Wytt hopped over to Ellayne and pulled at her bonds. Jack crawled to her. Between them, they woke her.

"Jack?"

"It's all right," he said. "Lie still so I can untie you. That man put something in our tea to make us fall asleep, and then he tied us up."

"Where is he?"

"Shh! You'll see."

When Jack untied her and helped her to sit up, she yelped when she saw the dead body.

"Wytt did it," Jack said. "He must've waited till he fell asleep, then stabbed him through the eye with his stick. And I'd say it's a good thing he did."

"But he's dead—"

"And that's the end of him. Your father told you this

country's full of outlaws. I guess Hesket was one of them. He had something nasty in store for us. Sell us into slavery, I guess."

"He drugged our tea."

"He won't be doing it to anybody else. And we're the richer by a donkey."

They didn't want to stay there with Hesket. Having slept since midday, they thought it best to move on. The North Star would show them the way. Jack recovered his bag and gave Wytt a piece of bread. Before they started out again, Wytt yanked his stick from Hesket's eye and wiped it on the ground to clean it. Ellayne shuddered.

"It isn't going to be just a nice adventure, is it?" she said. "It's going to be hard, and other terrible things are going to happen, and we'll be lucky if we make it to the mountain, let alone all the way to the top."

Jack nodded. "I'm afraid so. But King Ozias always said he only came out alive through so many dangers because God was watching over him. Maybe He's watching over us, too. If He didn't mean for us to get there, He wouldn't have sent me the dream."

They paused to pray that it was so, and then went on. Jack led Hesket's donkey, and Wytt ran along beside him.

CHAPTER 15

To Lintum Forest

By the time Jack and Ellayne actually reached Lintum Forest, Martis had been in Ninneburky long enough to find out what he wanted to know and to write a report to the First Prester. This is what he wrote.

Martis to Lord Reesh, greetings—

I have questioned the parties involved, and I must tell your lordship that the two missing children are probably the most intelligent persons in this village.

The girl's father, the chief councilor, has sent horsemen up the river, working the roads along both banks, without them meeting with any sign of his daughter. He has also had militia searching the country round Oziah's Wood, to no avail.

He says his daughter has no knowledge of Scripture, but is of an adventurous spirit and has lately shown signs of discontent. The girl's mother is too overwrought to add to this. I am persuaded the girl simply ran off with the boy, for some reason known only to them.

The boy's teacher at the chamber house, one Ashrof, reciter, confesses that he taught the child something of the Scripture, which he ought not to have done. That he taught him the verse in Penda, to wit, Ozias and the bell; but that he never mentioned it until after the boy told him of his dream and craved an interpretation. The boy had the dream many times before Ashrof told him about the bell. Reciter claims that when the boy voiced an intention to climb Bell Mountain, he did everything in his power to dissuade him.

The boy's stepfather, a carter, by all accounts cares nothing for him and was unaware of the boy's intentions.

Your lordship may take it that the boy instigated this action. How the girl came to join him in it, no one seems to know. If the reciter is to be believed, and I believe the man is honest but not wise, the dream came to the boy many times before he ever heard the verse from Penda.

I believe the child outwitted the authorities here. Expecting that they would try to capture him, if only to save the girl, he was shrewd enough not to follow the river up to the mountains, nor to pass by Oziah's Wood. If he had, they would have had word of him by now.

I believe he went south, as that would offer his best chance of eluding the militia, and any witnesses. That being the only route the militia has not investigated, I shall commit myself to it tomorrow.

If there is a culprit in all this, other than the boy's imagination, it is the old reciter who interpreted the dream. Farewell from your obedient servant, Martis.

Martis handed the letter to the local prester, who promised to send it to the Temple by his swiftest courier.

"Don't bother to try to read it," Martis said. "It's written in a cipher known only to the First Prester and myself. If the children return before I do, hold them here for me. I'll want to question them."

As he saddled his horse, it gave Martis some pleasure to imagine his master's reaction to his letter.

"South?" he would cry; and his face would get red. "That's not the way to Bell Mountain! That is only the way to a bleak and terrible country, an utter wasteland. Has been since the Empire fell! No, no—anyone who wishes to go to the mountain must follow the river."

Lord Reesh knew the Commentaries, the New Books written in the days just after the Empire fell. He would surely be thinking of one passage in particular, in the Annals of Olf: *And gouts of fire fell on the cities of the southern plain, devouring them all in a night, and burning off the pasturelands so that no life remained to bird or beast.* The land between Lintum and the great river, dotted with lifeless ruins, had lain desolate ever since. No one lived there. No one tried to.

The boy and the girl wouldn't know that: they wished only to avoid being dragged back to Ninneburky. Martis was impressed by the efforts of the chief councilor's militia. They hadn't encountered the children in the north or in the east. Therefore, the children weren't there. Unless they were headed west toward Obann itself, they must have gone south.

Martis checked his provisions and prepared to follow them.

Following their encounter with Hesket the Tinker, both Ellayne and Jack found themselves a prey to dark thoughts, which they didn't share.

Ellayne kept wondering what Hesket would have done to them if Wytt hadn't killed him. Naturally, she had no knowledge of the truly terrible things that certain kinds of persons might do to children if they had them in their power. It wasn't something her family would have discussed in front of her. All she had were some vague bits from various adventure stories, and those were bad enough. She'd read of witches who pitched children into ovens, cooked them, and ate them, and of outlaws who sold girls and boys over the mountains to the Heathen to be enslaved for the rest of their lives or used in human sacrifices. If she had known the things her father knew, but hadn't told her, she might not have gone any farther. But she didn't know, and so she kept up with Jack and the donkey as they plodded across the plain.

Jack had not lived as sheltered a life as had Ellayne. Van sometimes spoke of evil things he'd seen and heard of on the road (especially after he'd had his beer). Jack knew all along that there were people on the loose who did vile things. His plan was always to avoid them.

What worried him were things he didn't know about, and couldn't know until they overtook him. That a little creature like Wytt could kill a grown man was a revelation to him. What if they met Omahs who weren't friendly, who'd slay them as they slept? What other kinds of creatures were at large in the world, bigger and deadlier than the Omahs? Van hated to drive by night, on account of the strange noises that he heard. What made those noises? And what about the things that didn't make noise?

They plodded on, camped one more night on the open plain, and toward noon the next day won their reward: the sight of a solid rampart of trees blocking the way to the south, stretching east and west farther than the eye could see.

"There it is," Jack said. "Now we have to decide how close we want to be to the forest before we turn east to the mountains."

"A lot closer," Ellayne said, "in case we want to duck in and hide. But not too far in—we'll want to duck back out again."

"One thing we ought to do first is lighten this donkey's load," Jack said. "We probably don't need all this stuff."

"I'd just as soon not keep any of that man's things."

Going through the donkey's pack, they discarded Hesket's tea; some wrapped meat that had gone bad; a smelly old cloak; a pair of boots that needed mending; a bagful of black, malodorous chewing weed; and some pans and a kettle that were too filthy to be cleaned. Jack found a long, wicked-looking knife, almost a short sword, that Ellayne wanted to throw away, but he decided to keep. They kept the least soiled of a pair of blankets, some air-dried meat, and Hesket's waterskin, which was much larger than theirs.

Ellayne looked at the pile of discarded things and shook her head. "I suppose this stuff was all he had," she said. "I wonder what kind of life he had."

"He drugged our tea and tied us up—bogs on his life!" Jack said. "Come on, let's load up and get closer to the forest."

By the end of the day they were near enough to smell the trees when the breeze came from the south. The forest threw clusters of small trees out onto the plain, as if to contend with it for the territory. Around these trees the grass was green, there were bushes with purple leaves, and choruses of birds chirped, sang, and cawed.

"It's a much nicer country already," Jack said. "We can make a good camp here. Tomorrow, we head for the mountains."

In a grassy hollow sheltered by a stand of white birches, they made their camp and built their fire. They hungered for fresh meat, but hadn't had any since Jack shot the long-legged bird three days ago. Their bread was getting stale, but by now they'd eaten almost all of it. Jack wondered how they'd get on when their bread was gone, if he didn't get a lot better at hunting. And it was too early in the year for berries.

He worried about Ellayne's mood. He wanted to be happy because they'd completed an important part of their journey, but he couldn't be cheerful while she was so glum. He tried to snap her out of it by asking her to tell him a story, but she said she didn't feel like it. They might have stewed all night, had not sheer weariness sent them both to sleep.

Ellayne shook Jack awake at the first grey light of morning, and shook him hard.

"Jack! Jack! Wake up!"

"What's the matter?"

She was beaming. "Nothing's the matter! Except I've had the dream. Your dream! I dreamt I was home, and I went out the back door and looked up at Bell Mountain—and I heard it sing. Oh, Jack! You would've thought the sound would crack the sky. The bell must be as big as a house! But do get up, Jack. Let's get an early start—it's still a long way to the mountain."

CHAPTER 16

The Hermit

Ellayne went on about her dream all morning, and Jack soon enough got tired of it. He wished she'd be quiet long enough for him to get a shot at something, rather than scare all the game into hiding with her prattle. He'd had the dream first, anyway.

Wytt was somewhere nearby, always just out of sight, but Jack could hear him making all kinds of noise. What had gotten into him? Jack had a stone in his slingshot, ready to let fly if only he had something to shoot at.

The fringe of the forest seemed the right place for it. Somehow Jack couldn't bring himself to shoot any of the little songbirds that welcomed him to their country. He saw some bright red cappies with their black masks, and blue bawns, and once a bold yellow jerbee: the same birds he knew from the woods and fields of home. There were blackberry thickets all around, and things rustling and peeping and pattering in them—things that might be good to eat, if you could get a shot at them. Too bad it was much too early in the year for berries.

Wytt let out a shriek, and something else whooped back at him, and the brambles thrashed noisily, and an animal hopped out with Wytt in hot pursuit. It turned to snarl at him, and Jack knocked it over with a stone—he was really too close to miss. Wytt leaped onto it and skewered its side with his stick.

"We've got our supper!" Jack cried, overjoyed because he hadn't missed his shot.

"What did you get?" Ellayne asked, bringing up the rear with the donkey.

Jack wasn't sure. He bent over for a closer look. The animal lay quivering, breathing out its last breath. Wytt chattered at it. Ellayne came up while Jack was still trying to decide what it was.

"What kind of peculiar animal is that?"

"I was hoping you could tell me," Jack said.

It was about the size of a big tomcat, but with long hopping back feet like a rabbit's, and long ears like a rabbit's, too. But it had a long, straight tail, and no animal Jack knew had a tail like that, and short forelegs—and a long, delicate snout that was the last thing to stop moving when it died. Its soft brown fur was dappled with white spots down the back and flanks, like a fawn's.

"I've never seen a picture of anything like this," Ellayne said. "Do you think it's safe to eat?"

"We don't have much choice. I don't much care for that dried meat we found in Hesket's pack. I wonder if this is some kind of rabbit."

"With a nose like that? And a long tail?"

"It hopped like a rabbit."

"Then I hope it tastes like one."

Jack picked up the carcass; no point in killing it if they weren't going to eat it.

"It's a pretty thing, whatever it is," Ellayne said.

While the children hiked along the edge of Lintum

Forest, with the mountains before them, Ashrof sat quietly in his own front room. The prester had told him not to come back to the chamber house, so he had nowhere to go.

But that wasn't what he was thinking about.

Ashrof had lied to everyone—to the man from Obann, to the prester, to the chief councilor, and even to Jack. He'd lied by not telling anyone, not even Jack, that he'd had the dream, too. He'd heard Bell Mountain sing.

Lord Reesh would have understood why Ashrof hadn't wanted to tell anyone about the dream. Reesh knew the verse in the Book of Prophet Ika. *The least among you shall dream dreams: the boy and the maiden, the shepherd and the slave, the widow, the fatherless, and the old who are no more honored by the young.* Ashrof knew it well, and knew its meaning.

It was the call of God.

He shall visit His people with judgment.

It means the end of everything, Ashrof thought. No recovery this time. We've had a thousand years, since God brought down the Empire, to put our house in order, and we haven't done so. We've put aside the Scriptures, and the Temple is an empty house, devoid of faith. We spent a hundred years rebuilding it, and it's empty. We've had a thousand years to bring the people back to God, and we've only let them drift further and further away.

Ashrof never doubted Jack would get to the top of Mount Yul and find Ozias' bell and ring it. What would happen then? Would the earth crack wide open and swallow itself? Would the sky be shattered into pieces?

I should not have tried to hold him back, Ashrof thought, shouldn't have lied to him. He was going to go up no matter what I said because God had called him. I should have told him the truth. My poor Bucket. He's gone anyway, and he'll never come back.

May God forgive my weakness. My long life has made me but a coward.

Jack and Ellayne had the long-snouted creature for supper: sweet, firm meat, and plenty of it. Wytt gorged himself on tail meat, eaten raw. They were all in a good mood now.

"I just thought of something," Jack said. "As long as we can see Bell Mountain, we can never lose our way. And as it's the highest mountain, and the only one with a cloud on top, we'll never lose it. It'd be too bad to climb the wrong mountain!"

Night at the edge of the forest was a lot livelier than night on the plain. Owls hooted in the trees, and somewhere, farther into the woods, but not too far, a chorus of frogs broke out.

"Spring's here for good, if frogs are calling," Jack said. "Cold for spring, but the frogs wouldn't be out if it were still winter. You know, back home there's a boggy place not far from the river where you can't put your foot down at night without stepping on a frog."

"So that's what it is!" Ellayne said. "I always thought it was night birds when I listened to it from my bed. I never knew it was frogs. No one ever told me."

"They come out in the spring to lay their eggs."

Talking about frogs and birds, and spring and summer, they fell asleep early. But they woke early, too—jarred out of sleep by another kind of noise.

Jack was having a silly dream in which he was back home in his bed, watching a mob of fat hogs squeezing into his room, grunting and whuffling. When he opened his eyes, his room was gone, but he still heard the hogs.

Beside him Ellayne was already sitting up, staring out at the plain. Above her, tethered to a sapling, the donkey snorted nervously. Ellayne clutched Jack's arm and pointed. He sat up and looked.

"What are they?" she whispered.

The light was grey and watery with wispy drifts of mist rising from the grey grass of the plain; the sun had not yet risen over the mountains.

Out on the plain loomed large, dark forms. They were big—at least as big as bulls, Jack thought. But they weren't any kind of cattle. They had high, bulky shoulders; and backs that sloped down; forelegs quite a bit longer than their hind legs; and long, horsey heads. There were at least half a dozen of them, and they grunted and rumbled as they came. For once Wytt was quiet; he perched on Ellayne's lap, his little flat nose wrinkling feverishly.

"They're coming our way!" Ellayne said. "What'll we do?"

They came on slowly but steadily, with a very peculiar gait—it almost seemed to Jack that they were walking on their knuckles. One of them paused at a sapling; reached up with a long, powerful foreleg; and grappled the stem with a set of huge, curved, heavy claws. It pulled the tree down easily and devoured the leaves at the top.

The donkey began to tug against his tether.

"We'd better get out of their way—as far out as we can," Jack said.

They got up and hurriedly collected their things. Breakfast would have to wait. Jack got a firm grip on the donkey's lead before untying him from the tree. The poor beast rolled its eyes and showed the whites, gamely fighting off panic. "Easy now, easy, boy!" Jack said.

The big animals came closer. One sweep of those claws, Jack thought, and we've had it.

Leading the donkey, they fled into the forest, following whatever paths and openings presented themselves. It was dark under the trees, easy to bump into things. But they kept on until they couldn't hear the grunting and the rumbling anymore. They listened for the sound of heavy bodies in the underbrush; but it was quiet now, except for the song of birds greeting the new day, and sunlight had begun to find its way to the forest floor.

"I think we've lost them," Jack said.

"Did you see those claws?"

They'd come to a stop in a small clearing with brambles all around and a few enormous old oaks towering above them.

"What kind of animal has claws like that?" Ellayne said. "I suppose a bear might, but those things weren't bears—were they? I don't want to run into any bears!"

"Then you shouldn't have come to the forest," said a man.

The children startled. There stood a man at the opposite end of the clearing, barely twenty paces from them, looking like he'd been there all along.

"Don't be afraid," he said. "I'm all alone, and I serve God."

He wore a coarse cloth robe that reached down to his ankles, and sturdy leather sandals on his feet. He carried no weapon. His face was almost hidden in a squirrel's nest of grey hair and beard; but his blue eyes, Ellayne thought, looked frank and kindly.

"My name is Obst," he said. "I live alone out here in a cabin I built with my own hands. I came here many years ago to meditate and pray. You needn't be afraid of me."

That's what Hesket would've said, Jack thought. But now he had Hesket's big knife handy in the donkey's pack.

The man smiled at them. He spoke gently.

"Come," he said, "even a hermit is happy to have visitors sometimes. Come to my house and rest a spell. I'm sure you've had a long journey."

"How do we know you're really a hermit, and not an outlaw?" Jack said.

Obst laughed. "I don't know how to answer that! You must take me as you find me, I suppose. If you'd rather I left you alone, I shall. I can only say that I am what I appear to be and that I'll help you if I can."

"Let's go with him, Jack," Ellayne said. "Hermits are often very wise."

"As to that, Miss, I couldn't say. You'll decide for yourselves how wise I am," Obst said.

He did look harmless, Jack thought. He looked around for Wytt, but didn't see him. Well, that was all right: the Omah would stay close and help them if they needed him.

"We've already met one outlaw," Jack said.

"I look forward to hearing all about it."

Jack made up his mind. "All right—we'll come with you," he said. Obst reminded him of Ashrof, and that made Jack warm to him.

CHAPTER 17

The Man Who Missed God

Obst's cabin blended into the woods around it, almost as if it had grown there, and not been built. Jack didn't even see it at first. Moss grew on the door, creepers clung in sheets to the walls, and plants grew all over the roof—green grass and even a few small saplings.

"It's beautiful!" Ellayne said. "But why do you let those plants grow over it?"

"Winter nights have gotten colder since I first came here," Obst said, "and the summer days are hot. But inside my house, it never gets too cold or too hot. I find it very snug and cozy when snow covers it."

"How long have you lived here?" she asked.

He wrinkled his brow. "I don't think I can tell you that," he said. "A long time—that's all I know. I long ago stopped counting the days, the months, the years. All I can say for sure is that Lord Folcwan was First Prester when I came out here. I don't remember what year it was. But come inside now. I'll leave the door ajar, and you can hitch your donkey to it."

The cabin had two windows, so it wasn't too dark inside. There was only one room, but it was almost as much space as Van had in the four rooms of his house, Jack thought. This space had a hard dirt floor, swept clean, and a stone hearth and stone chimney. Bunches of herbs dangled from the beams that supported the ceiling, and in one corner lay a deep pile of fresh ferns that Jack supposed was the hermit's bed. What the walls were made of, he couldn't tell; they were plastered with clay.

There was a table with a chair and a three-legged stool. Obst must have made them himself. Jack saw tools hanging from pegs on the wall, and in another corner, an axe and a broom. There were also shelves on the wall, and these held clay jars, mugs, and plates—unpainted, unglazed, obviously made by the hermit as he needed them.

"Are you hungry?" Obst asked.

"We haven't had our breakfast," Jack said.

"Then you might enjoy my squirrel and mushroom stew. I'll heat it up for us. Sit down wherever you please."

Ellayne sat on the bed of ferns. Jack tried the chair, and found it solid and sturdy. Obst had an iron kettle on a tripod in the fireplace. He started a low fire under it with his tinderbox, and the smoke went up the chimney.

"We didn't have our breakfast," Jack said, "because some big animals were coming straight for our camp." He described them as best he could. "We never saw animals like that before, and they scared us off. What were they?"

Obst stirred the contents of the pot. "Yes—fierce-looking, aren't they?" he said. "They live in the forest by day and venture out onto the plain by night. They're harmless—although I once saw one disembowel a bear that had attacked them. Those claws can kill.

"As to what they are—well, I don't think anybody knows. Very few people live in these parts. I never saw those animals until a year or two ago, or maybe three, and I don't know where they came from. They seem to like it here, so I suppose they'll stay. There is no name for them. I've come to think of them as knuckle-bears because they look a little like bears and walk on their knuckles so as not to dull their claws. I've grown accustomed to them, and they to me."

The stew was beginning to smell good, much better than anything I could cook over a campfire, Jack thought.

"Aye, there's been many a change in the world lately," Obst said as he stirred. "Animals that no one has a name for, and not all of them peaceful like the knuckle-bears—that's only part of it. But finding the pair of you in my woods, two children alone, was the biggest surprise I've had in a long time. Where do you come from?"

Jack didn't want Ellayne telling any daft stories that came out of her books, so he tried to get in first with "Up north." But at the same time he spoke, she said, "Obann City." He glared at her, and her cheeks reddened.

"Can't agree on what to tell me, eh?" Obst said. "It shows you have reason to be cautious, and that you don't quite trust me. Very cautious indeed—a girl trying to look like a boy." That jolted Ellayne. "You don't trust me. Well, I don't blame you for that. Here, your stew's ready."

He spooned them each a generous portion in brown clay bowls that had hardened with his fingerprints still on them: an artistic potter he was not. He had no table utensils; Jack had to fish his own out of his pack. But the stew was warm and hearty, and the hermit insisted that they eat as much as they liked.

"I can always make more," he said. "Here in the forest, I want for nothing. There's a spring of sweet water nearby, and my snares are never empty. There's always plenty of food, once you've learned how to get it. I'll stay here until I come to the end of my days."

"But don't you get lonely?" Ellayne asked. "Don't you miss your family and your friends? And just being around other people?"

Obst leaned against his plastered wall.

"We all miss something in our lives," he said. "Yes—I still miss people. Sometimes I miss them very much. That's why I'm glad you're here. But when I lived among people in the city, I missed God. And that was worse than missing people."

Traveling on horseback, Martis made good time across the empty land. Only it wasn't as empty as he'd expected.

Unlike the children, he didn't camp on the hilltops at night. He knew they weren't natural hills, but all that remained of giant ruins, which more than a thousand years of rain, wind, ice, and the heat of the sun had ground down into the semblance of hills. But he did like to climb them to get a better view of what lay ahead.

No people inhabited this vast land, but he was surprised to find so many animals and birds. These included many kinds he'd never seen before, and he was a well-traveled man.

He knew from reports Lord Reesh had received that the few people living in the Northern Wilds had seen strange animals. No one crossed the River Winter anymore, not even the most intrepid fur trappers. They couldn't stand the cold winters and the heavy snows, and the fierce beasts that were multiplying in those regions. And this winter, some of the beasts came south, crossing the frozen river. There were tales of huge, fearsome shapes half-seen through the grey curtain of a blizzard. As far as Martis knew, no one had been killed. "Because they ran away too fast!" Lord Reesh said.

These southern plains attracted no settlers, no trappers: people didn't even cross them. There were no stories coming out of this country. When the Empire fell, God blasted it; and people stayed out of it.

So Martis was surprised to see long-legged birds hunting snakes and rodents in the grass, and animals like mice the size of dogs. Clearly God hadn't blasted the country forever. From where Martis sat in his saddle, it didn't look blasted. He wondered what Reesh would say about it. Maybe some settlers ought to be sent here.

Martis didn't tarry. If the children he sought were still alive, they would cross the empty country until they came up against Lintum Forest, and then turn east toward the mountains. There was no other way that they could go. Any hope he had of picking up their trail would have to wait until he reached the forest. There were people there. Eventually someone would see the children and tell him about them.

He rode on, careful not to overtax his horse.

Before the children could finish their breakfast, it began to rain. You could tell at a glance that it was going to be one of those rains that went on and on all day.

"You won't want to be traveling in this," said the hermit. "Unload your donkey while I fix him a shelter where he won't be too uncomfortable."

What else could they do? Jack arranged Hesket's blanket and a few other things so he could sit on it comfortably—and reach quickly under the pile and pull out the big knife, if he had need of it. Outside, right next to the cabin, Obst tied down some little trees to form a leafy canopy under which the donkey could rest without getting too wet. When he came back in, he shut the door but left the windows open.

"I can shutter them if the weather gets very bad," he said, "but I don't think it will. This is a spring rain, good for growing things. We'll keep the fire going and have some more stew later."

"You must have a very peaceful life, as a hermit," Ellayne said. "What made you decide to be one?"

"I told you. I missed God." Obst moved his stool closer to the fire and perched on it. It didn't wobble. "You're too young to have felt as I felt. I was a young man then, in the service of the Temple. I used to dream that I might become First Prester one day, by the time I was an old man. Now I'd rather be as I am."

He told a story that Jack thought much too long and very hard to follow. But his interest perked up suddenly when Obst stood up and laid his hand on something on one of his shelves.

"Do you know what this is?" he said, as the rain dripped off the leaves around the windows. "This is the very Book of Scripture that I took from the presters' library the day I left the Temple. This is my reason for being in this place. It is my whole reason for being.

"You might say I stole it. That would be true, up to a point. But they certainly weren't making any use of it in the library, and I doubt they ever missed it."

"Please, sir—read us some of it!" Jack said.

Obst looked surprised. "What's this? A boy who knows the Scripture?"

"Oh, I don't know it at all," Jack said. "But I would dearly like to hear it. I've always wondered what the Scriptures were really like. The prester at our chamber house never read to us from the Old Books. I had a teacher who said I was too young for it."

"I'm surprised you know the Old Books exist," the hermit said. "Very well, I'll read you some."

He sat down with the heavy book on his lap, and opened it carefully. A musty smell crept into the room. He handled the reed-paper pages delicately.

"*Su spakis Miklen Gotte, Ye schell niht maachen ayn hoos yff braas, butt Ih woll brayken ytt mauger syne coop,*" he read, and a good deal more. Jack thought, no wonder Ashrof said I wasn't ready for it. He didn't understand a word. And yet if he closed his eyes and just listened, without trying to make sense of it, he was sure he almost understood it. Understanding lay just out of reach.

Reading the verses aloud did something strange to Obst. He seemed to forget Jack and Ellayne were there. His eyes focused on something that they couldn't see, and he talked to himself—certainly not to them.

"I have seen the gathering of God's wrath," he said. "Winter is colder, and lasts longer. Uncouth beasts walk the earth, and lawless men multiply their numbers; and no crime is too foul for them because they know the end is near.

"The Temple is a house of whoredoms, and the presters think only of filling its treasuries with silver and gold. Do they think that will save them? Will God spare them for their robes of office? They wear white ermine, but their hearts are black with filthiness! Will they stand, when the bell is rung and all else is brought low?"

"The bell!" cried Ellayne.

Obst startled like a man rudely awakened from a light sleep. He stared at her.

"The bell on Bell Mountain—is that the one you mean?" she said. "But that's where we're going!"

Jack could have stuffed a mittful of ferns into her mouth, if only he'd been sitting next to her. He gritted his teeth and scowled at her, but she didn't look at him. Why wouldn't she shut up?

"You shouldn't have told him!" he said.

Ellayne's mouth popped open, but no more words popped out.

"Wait—don't fight!" Obst said. He closed the book with great care and returned it to the shelf. "You have nothing to fear from me, children. You can be sure I always knew you weren't wandering around these parts for any ordinary reason.

"Now that you've let it slip out, why not tell me everything? I've done nothing all my life, since I left the Temple, but study the Scripture. Who better to advise you? It's raining, you can't travel—you might as well trust me. For I believe God Himself brought you here to me. You won't meet anyone else in all the land who'll say that to you."

Ellayne, whose face had gone quite pale, looked pleadingly to Jack.

"Please, Jack, let's tell him!" she said. "Hermits are holy men. He won't hurt us."

And where did you learn so much about hermits? snarled Jack, inwardly. In those daft books of yours, I guess! But we're not in a book. We're here in this man's house, and he's half mad.

"I can at least tell you where the outlaws are, and how to avoid them," Obst said.

"If you know where they are, then they must know where you are—and they've done no harm to you," Jack said. "Why should that be, unless you're one of them?"

Obst smiled. "Look around, child. Do I have anything worth stealing? Besides, some of them come to me when they're sick or hurt. I have the gift of healing. They have no reason to hurt me. And the Most High protects me, even as He has protected you, so far.

"But if you wish to tell me no more about yourselves, so be it. Leave whenever you please. I'll do you no harm, and help you all I can."

Jack looked him over, as if a lie might break out like a rash on his skin. He wished he knew where Wytt was. He wished he knew whether to trust this man. Who else could tell them what it said in Scripture?

"All right," he said. "Tell us first about the beasts. And then we'll tell you about the bell."

CHAPTER 18

"It Was in My Heart to Slay You"

In the tales of Abombalbap, hermits were always wise and good, true holy men. A few of them could even make miracles. That was why Ellayne wanted badly to tell Obst everything, and was so happy when Jack finally agreed.

But as Jack began to speak of his dreams, and how the mountain sang to him, the rain came down a little harder, and the room inside the cabin became a little darker. Ellayne found herself thinking that maybe they shouldn't have trusted this hermit after all. He looked like he was intently listening to every word Jack said; but when you looked again, you could see it was more like he was listening to something else that you couldn't hear. Jack noticed it and stopped talking; but Obst didn't stop listening.

"Master hermit—are you all right?" Ellayne asked, after several long moments of silence.

His lips moved. Jack got up and came a few steps closer to him.

"I think he's reciting Scripture," he told Ellayne. "But it's in the language of the Old Books. I can't understand what he's saying."

"I wonder if there's something wrong with him," Ellayne said.

Jack did an odd thing then. He picked up the hermit's axe and tossed it out the window. Obst didn't seem to notice.

"What'd you do that for?"

"I wish I had some rope," Jack said. "I'd tie him up. I think he might be about to go mad."

"Well, then—maybe we'd better leave before he does."

At that moment Wytt jumped onto the window ledge where the axe had just gone out. He startled the children, making them flinch. He stood there, looking in, and chattered loudly at them. Obst heard that. He turned on his stool to see him, stared at Wytt and sighed.

"And the hairy ones shall inherit all those cities," he recited. Rising, he went to the hearth and got a ladleful of stew and held it out toward Wytt, making squirrel noises at him. Wytt hopped onto the floor, boldly approaching the hermit. Obst lowered the ladle. Wytt dipped his fingers into the stew and licked them. Obst stood still so he could eat, and turned to smile at Jack. It wasn't a mad smile at all.

"So you've made a friend, eh? One of the Omah," he said. "Very, very good! I wish you'd told me—although I might not have believed you."

"I was coming to it," Jack said. "But then you drifted off and started talking to yourself in Scripture. You weren't listening to anything we said."

"We thought something bad might've happened to you," Ellayne said.

"Not bad," Obst answered. Wytt went on eating stew. "Sometimes I'll be praying or meditating in the morning, and the next thing I know, night has fallen, and I'm stiff and hungry. It's something God does, when you're close to Him."

Wytt finished his meal. Obst straightened his back and stretched, and Wytt hopped over to sit on Ellayne's lap.

"Just so you understand me," Obst said, "I have a confession to make to you.

"It was in my heart to slay you—to stop you from climbing the mountain and ringing the bell. I, who have sought God all my life, was afraid. I was desperately afraid. All my years of prayer and study, and obedience—they were as nothing. All swallowed up in fear! And that was when I stopped hearing you."

Ellayne's heart did a flutter, and she saw Jack glance at the corner where the axe had rested.

Obst held up a hand. "I'm not telling you this to scare you!" he said. "God took away my fear. I couldn't hear you, couldn't see you, because God took me away for a little time and changed my heart. And now I understand what He wishes me to do.

"If you'll have me, I'll come with you. The forest is my home; I'll be a good guide. I'll help you every step of the way—even to the top of the mountain, if we get that far, as I believe you will, whether I do or not."

Ellayne knew Jack had the big knife under the blanket he was sitting on. He kept his right hand very close to it.

"And what happens to us if you change your mind again?" he said.

"If I were planning to harm you, I wouldn't put you on your guard against me, would I?" Obst said. "I think we ought to leave tomorrow and stay within the forest all the way to the skirts of Bell Mountain. We won't have to spend much time in open country. With me to guide you, and decent weather, we can be there in two or three weeks. But maybe you ought to discuss it between yourselves. I'll go out and get us some fresh water from the spring."

He took up a big clay jar and went out the door, leaving it ajar.

"Let's get out of here before he comes back," Jack said.

"But Jack—he knows the way."

"He's crazy."

He started gathering up their things, and Ellayne had to help him. They made fast work of it, loaded the donkey, and led him off through the woods, trying to find the way back to the plain.

But they couldn't find it. Jack thought he knew how to find his way around in the woods because he played in the woods at home in Ninneburky. Now he realized that experience didn't count. Those were only little wooded patches, after all: walk ten minutes in any direction, and you were out.

He tried to lead the way, but he didn't remember anything about the paths they'd followed to get to Obst's cabin or the trees they'd passed. Everything looked different in the afternoon, and it was still raining, too.

"This is awful!" Ellayne cried. "Where are we going?"

"Away from Obst, as far as we can," Jack said. At least it was true.

They were on a path and had to follow wherever it led. Sometimes it narrowed, and they were brushed by rain-soaked underbrush. Their clothes got soggy. The donkey came along quietly enough, and Wytt raced ahead of them, occasionally whistling.

Then, suddenly, the donkey dug his hooves in, and Jack had a fall. He kept his hold on the lead and scrambled back up.

The poor little ass had his ears laid back and the whites of his eyes showing and his teeth. Jack felt his own hair stand on end. Ellayne clung to the donkey's pack.

"Steady, boy, steady!" Jack tried to soothe the donkey. If he really did bolt, Jack doubted they could hold him. And if he ran away with all their things …

The donkey drew back his lips and groaned.

Ahead of them, a patch of tall ferns waved back and forth, and they heard footfalls.

The ferns parted, and out came something that froze Jack's mind.

It was an animal, a big one, much, much bigger than a man, bigger even than a horse, though not so tall. It was brown, mostly, with a long, straight tail of a lighter shade of brown, and vivid black and white stripes up and down its flanks. Its head was something like the head of a dog with rounded ears. But it couldn't possibly be a dog because of what it carried in its jaws—the head, neck, shoulder, and foreleg of a knuckle-bear, with the long leg and curved claws dragging on the ground. The huge trophy was held in those jaws as easily as the carcass of a pheasant in the jaws of a big hunting dog. How wide those jaws gaped to hold it! The knuckle-bear's heavy, horse-like head lolled, but didn't touch the ground.

The beast paused for a moment to study them with a pair of yellow eyes, then crossed the path and disappeared into the high ferns on the other side. Jack and Ellayne waited for a long time in the rain, but it didn't come back.

It was Ellayne who found her voice first, and she got Jack's attention by hitting him on the shoulder with her fist.

"I don't care how crazy Obst is!" she said. "We've got to go back. We're soaking wet, it'll be night soon, and if you think we ought to stay out here all night, you're crazier than he is!"

Jack fended off another blow. "All right, you're right—stop hitting me!" he said. "We'll turn right around and go back."

The donkey trembled, huffing and puffing; but he didn't resist when they turned him, and didn't at all mind going back. He was an awfully good donkey, Jack thought, and petted his wet, furry neck. Van's ox would've just bolted and never come back.

"Faster, Jack!" Ellayne said.

"I'm going as fast as I can."

He didn't know if they could find their way back to Obst's cabin. If they came to a fork in the path, he wouldn't know which way to go.

They didn't talk, but put all their efforts into going as fast as they dared. With the trees overhead coming into leaf, and the rain coming down, and the sky completely overcast, Jack had no idea how much time they had before night fell.

"We'll be lucky if we don't get sick," Ellayne said.

Up ahead, Wytt uttered a series of sharp little barks and piercing whistles. A moment later they saw him with the hermit following after. Obst wore a kind of cloak made of straw and a fur cap on his head.

"Ah—there you are," he said.

Ellayne ran a few steps toward him, but stopped short.

"Master Obst, we're sorry we ran away. We were afraid of you," she said.

"It's all right," he said.

"We saw a horrible animal!"

"You'd better come back with me and get warm," the hermit said. He smiled, looking better when he smiled. "In truth, you didn't get very far. And you're safe." He looked at Jack. "Are you ready to come back to my house?"

Jack felt like he'd lost a fight. He nodded. "I reckon we are," he said.

"I have a kind of tea made from blackberry leaves," Obst said. "It'll do you good. And you need to sit by the fire. Come."

He led them up the path. Jack wished they didn't have to go with him, but they had no choice.

CHAPTER 19

The Assassin and the Thieves

Having ridden through the rain all day, the next morning found Martis not far from Lintum Forest. Once he reached it, he could begin his hunt for the missing children.

But he turned aside that morning to investigate the behavior of some birds—buzzards, he thought—descending on something that lay out of his sight to the east. Anything sizeable that died on the plain, he thought, might turn out to be one or both of the children. In that case his journey would be over.

As he expected, he found buzzards and crows feeding on a carcass. There was another bird, too, as big as a stork, if not bigger, tearing at the corpse with a heavy hooked beak that reminded Martis of a turtle's jaws. This bird glared at him as he rode up, then turned and ran off at a speed any horse would be hard put to match.

Martis whooped and waved his hat, driving off the crows and buzzards. Now he could see what they'd been picking at.

It was all that was left of a man, and not much: no face, no hands. But from the condition of the dead man's clothes, he could not have been lying there for more than a few days. Scavengers had begun to tear away the clothing, but hadn't finished.

The smell made Martis' horse fidgety. He kept the animal under control.

He wondered what there was out here that could kill a man. He'd seen no dangerous animals. When a man lay dead and unburied, the reason usually was another man; but Martis hadn't seen another human being since leaving Ninneburky. There were outlaws in the forest, but what would bring them out onto the plain?

"Easy, there—easy," Martis whispered to his horse, as he dismounted. Holding the reins, he looked for tracks. What with all the rain yesterday and the plethora of bird prints, he couldn't find any.

There were clerics who would have at least blessed the corpse before moving on, but Martis wasn't one of them. He'd been with Lord Reesh too long to believe in blessings.

He rode only a little farther to the south when two men in buckskin stepped out from behind a stand of birches.

"Stop right there, you!"

The one held up his arms. The other carried a bow with an arrow on the string. He wasn't ready to shoot, and that was his undoing.

Martis plucked a sharp skewer from his cloak, and before the other man could pull his bowstring, the skewer thunked into his chest. He gave a loud cry, dropped his weapons, fumbled at the skewer without being able to get hold of it, and then pitched forward onto his face. The second man stared at him. He had a knife in one hand and a cudgel in the other, but seemed to have forgotten them for the moment.

"Drop your weapons and stand still," Martis said, "or I'll ride you down and bash out your brains." Under his cloak he had a mace hooked to his belt. It had an iron head with four sharp flanges, and now Martis brandished it in his hand. The man in buckskin took one look at it and obeyed.

"That makes two bodies lying dead on this uninhabited ground," Martis said. "I suppose you and your friend murdered the other fellow whom I found about a mile north of here. Robbed him, did you? As no doubt you hoped to rob me."

"Burn you—no!" the man cried, shaking his head. "That other fellow was a friend of ours, Hesket the Tinker. We don't know who killed him. But who are you, who comes riding a horse out here where no one ever rides? Hesket had a donkey, but whoever killed him took it."

Martis twitched his cloak aside to show the red and white braid on his shoulder. He seldom wore it, but he thought it might be useful to him in this mission.

"As you can see," he said, "I'm in the service of the Temple. I've come a long way, and I'm not in a good mood, so you'd be wise to try to please me. First tell me your names, and what you and your friend are doing here."

"Bless you, elder brother, we're thieves, my partner and I. That's Osrhy, who you've killed. Thieves we are, but no murderers. My name's Oolf.

"As for our being out here, well, our friend Hesket was to meet us, and he didn't turn up, so we went out to look for him in case he was hurt or something. We know the way he always goes, so we went out to find him. And find him we did, but too late to do him any good. When we saw you coming—not knowing you were from the Temple—we thought we'd try for your horse. I confess we meant to steal him from you. We wouldn't, if we knew you were from the Temple. And that's the truth, elder!"

Martis believed him, although he was a little surprised to find so much reverence for the Temple in a country that didn't have a chamber house, let alone a prester. He must remember to tell Reesh. But to move on to more important matters:

"Answer truthfully, Oolf," he said. "Have you seen or heard anything of two children traveling in this country? They would have come down from the north and crossed the plains."

"Children, elder?" The thief seemed genuinely puzzled. "Nay, I've not seen any children round these parts, traveling or otherwise. It'd be a very remarkable thing to see children around here, elder."

"Who do you think killed the tinker?"

"Bless me, sir, I don't know. There wasn't anyone I knew but liked Hesket and bartered with him. Nor do I reckon he'd be an easy man to kill, either. He was a very cautious sort of man and full of tricks."

"You're sure you've heard nothing of the two children?"

"Oh, very sure indeed!" Oolf said. Martis decided the thief was scared enough to be telling the truth.

"I'm a stranger in these parts, so perhaps you could advise me," Martis said. "If you were looking for two children who'd crossed the plains, but you weren't sure exactly where they'd crossed, where do you think they'd be most likely to be seen by people? If they came to the forest, say, and then turned east. Think carefully. I very much want to find them."

Oolf was beginning to think that he'd neither be killed nor sold into slavery if he answered all the questions honestly. That was just what Martis wanted him to think.

"Elder," he said, after a long pause, "there's one man in these parts who stays put and knows better than anybody what's what. He's a hermit named Obst, and he's been here longer than anyone can remember. Sooner or later, he gets all the news. His house is not far from here. I can tell you how to find it, if you like."

Martis thought it would be wise to consult the hermit. Oolf gave him directions to the hermit's cabin, and Martis repeated them to be sure he had them right.

"There's one more thing you can do for me, younger brother, before we part," he said. "Please retrieve my skewer from your partner's chest, wipe it clean, and hand it up to me—there's a good fellow."

Oolf obeyed; and when he held up the skewer, Martis took it with his left hand, and with his right, crushed the thief's skull with the iron-shod mace. Oolf went down without a murmur, dead before he hit the ground.

Martis dismounted to wipe his mace clean on Oolf's clothes. He stuck his skewer back into his cloak, mounted up again, and rode on, leaving two dead men behind him.

CHAPTER 20

The Dues Collector

Obst knew the forest like Jack knew the streets of Ninneburky. The paths he chose never petered out in the middle of a bramble patch, or a miry spot of ground. He taught the children how to make a good shelter in a few minutes, just by bending saplings into arcs, anchoring them to the ground, and piling leaves and ferns in the right places. He knew which mushrooms and tubers were good to eat and how to set up snares to catch his supper. Best of all, he knew how to start a fire without matches, needing nothing but a sharp stick, a chunk of rotten wood, and some dry duff from the forest floor—all of which you ought to keep ready to hand, in case it rained and you couldn't find anything dry. The first night out, he taught them and let them try to make fire; and Ellayne squealed with delight when she was the first to get a flame going. Trust girls to make a fuss, Jack thought.

So they had their fire, supper in their bellies, a leafy shelter over their heads, and dry leaves to nestle down in. And Obst sat on his heels and peered straight out into the night, and didn't say a word. His lips moved constantly, but the children couldn't hear anything.

"He's doing it again," Jack said. "I hope he's still our friend when he snaps out of it. I hope he doesn't change his mind again about killing us."

"Oh, stop it, Jack! He's praying."

"It's no kind of praying I ever saw in the chamber house. It isn't even the kind of prayer we did up on the hill that night; and I'm sure we weren't doing it the right way."

"Maybe we shouldn't be talking or making noise."

"He isn't listening. I don't think he can hear us."

It made them uneasy to share the shelter with someone who was doing something they didn't understand. Ellayne could hardly imagine what her father the chief councilor would think of Obst. And outside in the dark, unseen animals and birds made unearthly noises: a whoop here, a clatter there. Jack and Ellayne both thought of the horrific animal they'd seen carrying half of a knuckle-bear in its enormous jaws—thought of it, but didn't talk about it. Wytt crawled under Ellayne's coat and went to sleep in her lap. Tethered to a nearby tree, the donkey slept, too.

"We ought to give him a name," Ellayne said. Trying to name a donkey would be much better than just sitting there, waiting for who knew what.

"He's a good donkey. He deserves a good name," Jack said.

Ellayne wanted to give him a name out of a storybook—Gallaweyk, after Abombalbap's horse, or Lleffrew, after somebody who'd killed a one-eyed giant once. But Jack held out for the name of Ham, after an older boy who'd taught him how to make a slingshot. This time Jack got his way—and with it, a tiny pang of homesickness.

"I wish my father would've let me go out to the river and play with you and your friends," Ellayne said. "I wonder why he kept me home all the time!"

Just then Obst sighed and stretched his legs. He shifted

to a more comfortable position, cross-legged.

"You needn't stare," he said. "I've told you these spells are a gift God gives me. It's how He talks to me."

"God talks to you? What does He say?" Ellayne asked.

"He doesn't talk like we talk, in words. At least, if there are words, I don't remember them when it's over. I suppose if I were a prophet, such as prophets were of old, I might be able to remember them and repeat them to God's people. But I'm not a prophet. The words are in my heart, somehow, but not in my mind."

"How did you learn to do it?" Jack said.

"It isn't something you learn," Obst said. "It just started happening after I'd been out here for some years. I would read the Scripture, and meditate, and pray, and it was like a brook feeding into a larger stream. I don't suppose the brook knows how that happens. There it is, trickling along, and the next thing it knows, it's part of something greater."

"But who is God, really?" Ellayne said. "It's so confusing! Who is He?"

Obst stared at her. "What an extraordinary question!" he said. But Jack was glad she'd asked it.

"You say He talks to you, like a person, but without words," she said. "And in my books, presters and hermits and even knights are always talking about God, but they never say who He is or what He's like, or why they're interested in Him. People nowadays don't talk like that. They go to the chamber house on Assembly days and the prester says, 'God bless the nation of Obann,' or something like that, and nobody knows what it means."

"And I asked my teacher," Jack put in, "and he said I'd have to wait until I was old enough to read the Scriptures."

Obst shook his head. He put his hands over his eyes, then let them fall with a slap against his thighs.

"The world is worse now than it was in the days of the Empire's greatest wickedness!" he cried. "Children, you walk on God's earth under His sky. You breathe His air and drink His water!

"How could I begin to tell you who God is? An age upon an age ago, Obann was a holy people. In those days the Most High revealed the Scriptures to His people and spoke to them through prophets. God's words are with us still—but no one listens.

"Don't you see? That's why I came to Lintum Forest. I couldn't find God in the Temple that was built to His name. The presters didn't know Him. All God's people have forgotten Him, and He has turned His back on them. Worse! He shall destroy them!"

Tears shone on his face. Jack wondered why he wept. What had they said that was so terrible? Jack was very sure there was not a soul in Ninneburky who would cry over God. But the hermit was at least half a madman: no telling what would make him laugh or cry.

Obst took a very deep breath, then sat up straight and reined himself in.

"Your ignorance is not your fault," he said. "It's been a long, long time in Obann since children were taught the truth. So be it!

"I'll teach you, if I can. A little bit at a time, as we travel. That way you can take it in. I received little enough instruction as a child, and that was a long time ago. Now I suppose there's no instruction at all, but only the aggrandizement of the Temple in its greed for worldly things.

"Listen, then. To answer your question: yes, God is a person, even as each of us is a person. He made us that way.

"This is the most important thing for you to learn, children. Everything you see, and everything you can't see, from the stars in heaven to the stones under the ground, the animals, the plants, the sun and moon, and all the people who have ever lived, including you and me—all of that, God created.

"A potter takes clay and makes a pot. But God took Nothing and out of it made Everything."

He paused to smile at them. "Now don't tell me that you understand that! Because no one ever has understood it, and no one ever will—not fully. We can only go on trying to understand it for as long as we live.

"What I've just taught you is the very first thing in all the Scriptures and the oldest teaching in the world. If we can receive it, then we can receive everything else the Old Books have to offer.

"Now, settle down for the night and try to believe. Try to understand."

The next day they were up early and made good time through the woods, Obst leading the way with long strides; it was hard for the children to keep up. He'd spoken hardly a word since they woke, but Jack didn't suppose a hermit was used to talking, having lived alone for so long.

His silence was infectious. Jack and Ellayne hardly spoke to one another. Part of the reason was that Jack kept thinking about all the things the hermit said the last night, especially the bit about God making all the people out of nothing. He guessed Ellayne was thinking about it, too. What did it mean? You couldn't make something out of nothing; you always had to start with something else. But that's what the Old Books said God did. Jack wondered why neither Ashrof nor the prester had ever mentioned it.

He was pondering this when Obst, leading the way, stopped suddenly, thrusting out a hand to stop the others.

"Someone's coming!" he said. "Whoever it is, don't either of you speak. Not a word."

Jack heard men's voices. Just ahead lay a small open space, and two men were entering it from the opposite direction. They spotted Obst right away, and stopped. He lifted his walking-staff to greet them.

"Hello there, old man! Fine day for a ramble, eh?"

"Hello, Bort," Obst said. "I'm surprised to see you in these parts."

This was the first man to enter the clearing—a short, fat fellow, almost round, with a round face and a nose like a ball of dough. Most fat people looked soft, but everything about this man was hard—especially his eyes, Jack thought. The man behind him was younger, taller, thinner. Both were dressed in green from head to toe, in clothes much stained and often mended.

"Why shouldn't we be in these parts?" the younger man said.

"Quiet, Tumm!" fat Bort said. "I guess I know what you mean, old man. But why should I care where I go in all of Lintum Forest?"

"He means we're not afraid of Helki," said the younger man. Bort shot him a look that persuaded him to say no more.

"Why don't you tell us who your little friends are, Obst? It may be we can find a use for them."

"They're under my protection. I'm sure your master wouldn't want you to trouble us."

"I wouldn't call Latt Squint-eye my master. We're all free men in Lintum. But who said anything about trouble? We're all friends here," Bort said. "What news from your neck of the woods?"

By now Jack realized these were outlaws, and when he traded a look with Ellayne, he knew she realized it, too. He was glad Obst hadn't made them talk about Hesket.

"That looks like the tinker's donkey," Bort said. "How did you come by it? He'd never trade that beast, though he'd trade his own mother."

"It belongs to these children," Obst said.

"And when are you going to tell us who they are and what you're doing with them?" Tumm said.

"I'm taking them to their father, who's working in the mines at Silvertown," Obst said. "I'm sure you remember Latt has given me safe conduct anywhere in Lintum, since I healed the ulcer on his leg. I'm sure you're on your way somewhere to collect Latt's dues for him—but you won't get anything from Helki, except for a drubbing with his rod. I wouldn't spend much time around here if I were you. Hasn't he sworn to kill you?"

Both of the outlaws glowered fiercely.

"You can tell Helki when you see him that I don't care a snap for his threats." Bort snapped his fingers. "It so happens we are on our way somewhere else and only passing through. But you can tell Helki that one of these days Latt will hang him from the highest tree in the woods. Let's go, Tumm!"

Obst and the children made way for them, and they clumped off in a hurry. Obst led the way across the clearing and up the path down which the outlaws had come. He said nothing for perhaps an hour, then stopped and turned.

"That is Hesket's donkey, isn't it? I recognize it now," he said. "And you did mention that you'd already met one outlaw. I think you'd better tell me what happened."

"Those two men back there were outlaws, too—weren't they?" Jack said.

Obst nodded. "Bort the Collector is indeed an outlaw, and you're lucky I was with you when you met him. He works for Latt Squint-eye, who styles himself King of Lintum Forest. Most of the others pay dues to him, and Bort collects them. Those who don't pay come to bad ends.

"Hesket the Tinker doesn't work for Latt, but has always been very useful to him. He'll want to know how you came by Hesket's donkey. You'd better tell me."

He had to wait for his answer.

"We didn't kill him," Ellayne said.

"But he put something in our tea that made us go to sleep, and then he tied us up," Jack said. "It was nighttime when we woke, and he was already dead. And we couldn't just leave the donkey there."

Obst drew the whole story out of them, question by question. Wytt came out of the ferns and stood listening, as if he understood every word. But he didn't react when Jack told how Hesket died.

"God has provided you with a protector," the hermit said. "Well, well—the tinker was an amusing man and good company on a stormy night, but he deserved his fate. He would have sold you to the Heathen beyond the mountains—or worse. He should have protected you, but he chose to do evil.

"There is a brisk trade in human souls over the mountains these days. That's why there are so few settlers here, although the land is rich and fertile. In ancient times, in the days of the good kings, God's Law ruled in Lintum Forest. Not anymore! Only a mockery of law, imposed by the likes of Latt Squint-eye."

They made their camp late that day; night almost overtook them. Obst spoke again after they ate.

"I'd planned to take you to Silvertown before we turned north for Bell Mountain," he said. "Now it seems better for us to change course and turn sooner. I'd rather not trust in Latt's safe-conduct any more than I have to."

Somewhere in the dark—impossible to tell how far away—something let out a long, quavering wail. Ellayne shuddered.

"A wolf," Obst said. "Wait, and you'll hear it answered. There are more wolves in Lintum than there used to be."

Another voice took up the howl, and then another, and another. Soon a whole chorus filled the night.

"The world is getting worse, isn't it?" Jack asked.

Obst didn't answer. He sat stock-still, muttering Scripture under his breath.

"God's going to end the world when He hears the bell," Ellayne said. "He's going to put an end to the whole world, an end to everything. Maybe we shouldn't ring the bell."

But Jack found he couldn't even think of turning back.

"If God is strong enough to make the world, and strong enough to end it, I don't see why He'd need us to ring the bell before He does what He wants to do," Jack said. "And if it isn't us, it'll just be someone else. But if God wants me to ring the bell, I think I'd better. I'd be too afraid not to."

CHAPTER 21

A New Prophecy

Martis had started some days behind the children he sought; but he was on horseback, and he knew he must be catching up. He was so sure of it that when he came to the hermit's cabin and found it empty, he decided to wait a day or two for the hermit to come back. Compared to camping on the hard ground in the rain, the cabin was a haven. He'd traveled hard and needed rest.

He spent a night there and all of the next day. He was amazed to discover that the hermit had a whole Book of Scripture. A book like that, if it could be had at all, would cost a good deal of money. How had an impoverished hermit come by it?

Martis was a well-traveled man, but he'd never met a hermit; this would be his first. He wondered what would make a man, in this day and age, sequester himself in the woods with only the Scriptures for company. It was unusual enough hundreds of years ago, unheard-of now. He hoped he'd have some time to question the hermit about it.

It wasn't the hermit who came to the cabin on the evening of the second day, but two men together.

"Who's that in the cabin?" someone called. Martis had heard them coming, but hadn't come out to greet them. Now he did, with his skewer hidden in his hand in case he needed it.

"Who are you?" demanded a fat man with a hard face, when Martis appeared in the doorway.

"Why, a servant of the Temple, come in search of his spiritual brother," Martis said, displaying his red and gold braid. "I am disappointed to find him not at home. Perhaps you have news of him?"

"He's traipsing around in the forest—" the taller of the two men started to say; but the fat one swatted him in the belly, and he gulped back the rest of his words.

"I see by the way you eye my horse and my clothing that the pair of you are lawless men," Martis said. "Is everyone in Lintum Forest so? I would much prefer a peaceful visit and friendly relations all around. But I must tell you that the last two outlaws I encountered, who sought to steal my horse, are dead, and by my hand. Take that as a friendly warning."

The younger man's nostrils flared. He looked as if he'd like to put Martis to the test. But the fat man, older and more experienced, chose caution.

"I reckon I know a killer when I see one," he said. "Don't try anything funny, Tumm. Our elder brother here has killed more men than you and me together. It's in his eyes. Obann's a long way from here. They must've picked up some pretty strange habits in the Temple, nowadays, to employ a man like this.

"My name is Bort, elder brother, and this is Tumm. We're making our rounds, collecting dues for Latt Squinteye, the chief of all the free men in the forest. You must have heard of him."

"His fame has not spread to the inner chambers of the Temple, I regret to say," Martis answered. "Well! Now that we understand each other, why don't you come in and sit down? We can break bread together, and I'm sure you'll want to stay the night."

Bort grinned. "Just so we really understand each other—no tricks, eh?"

Martis smiled back at him. "I promise not to kill you unless you try to rob or kill me. As a servant of the Temple, I always keep my promises."

Obst that night taught Jack and Ellayne how God made the first man and woman and then peopled the whole world. It was all new and strange to them. But in olden days, he said, children learned these things before they learned to walk, and there wasn't a soul in Obann who didn't know this story.

First there was the Isle of Eness-Ateen, at the very center of the world: the spot where God's words first brought life up from the earth. From this place, the Navel, life spread out like ripples on the surface of a pond—but much, much faster—until it covered the surface of the world, and swam in the waters, and flew in all the skies.

"God made the man and woman last," Obst said, "and He kept them there on Eness-Ateen because it was the fairest single place in all the world. 'And you are the jewels in this My treasury,' He said to the Man and the Woman. And He gave them names; but they lost their names when they became disobedient."

God commanded them never to drink from the Spring that bubbled up from the ground in the center of the island, in exactly the spot where God's first word of life struck home. It was the only commandment that He gave them.

"Only one," said Obst, "and yet they disobeyed it. The Nameless One appeared in the form of a great worm and tempted them. 'Drink of that water but once,' said the worm, 'and you shall be as great as God, and He must give way to you.' So they drank: first the Woman, then the Man.

"But the worm had lied to them. That which is created can never become the Creator. When they drank that water, they drank only Fear and Confusion and Shame. And God cast them out of Eness-Ateen, and moved it upon the waters to another sea where no man shall ever find it or even come in sight of it. God took away their names and gave them new names, making them forget the old ones. And the Man's name was *Khash*, meaning Lost; and the Woman's name was Sorrow.

"God removed them to an island called Caha, which was a mighty island. There they had to learn to hunt, plant crops, and tend herds. There they had many children, and those had children of their own, until all Caha was populated. Lost and Sorrow died because they had been cast out of the Island of Life, but their descendants were very numerous.

"So a long age passed," Obst said, "and the people of Caha learned wickedness and violence because the Nameless One came often among them, in many disguises, and they always listened to him. They hated God because He had cast them out of Eness-Ateen and taken it away from them, and they had to work for their food and suffer heat and cold and weariness, and in the end, they died.

"Only one man, Geb, still loved God and never listened to the Nameless One. He had more children than any other man, and he taught them all to be faithful to the Most High.

For this the people hated the Children of Geb and plotted to murder them and offer their blood as a sacrifice to devils.

"For this reason God sank the entire land of Caha under the waves of the sea and drowned every living thing; but the Children of Geb He enabled to walk upon little islands like stepping-stones all the way to the mainland. And there they became the ancestors of all the nations of men. As for the stepping-stone islands, God removed them so that no one could ever find a way back to the place where cursed Caha once rose above the waves.

"That's enough for now," Obst said. "I've greatly shortened the tale in my telling. Someday you ought to read it in the Scriptures."

Jack and Ellayne had questions, dozens of them.

"I thought all the stories were in storybooks!" Ellayne said. "I never knew the Old Books had stories, too."

Obst gave her a stern look. "These are not *stories*," he said. "They are the record of what was, and the explanation of what is, and signs for what shall be. They are the Word of God, transmitted through His prophets. They are to be taken seriously, and believed."

Jack had so many questions that he couldn't get one out. Ashrof, he remembered, had sometimes mentioned the Children of Geb and the drowning of Caha. But why hadn't Ashrof ever told him the whole story?

He did manage to blurt out something.

"What happened to the Nameless One? I never heard of him! What was he? And why did God punish the people and not him?"

"Oh, ho! I'd be up all night trying to answer that question," Obst said. "There's no short answer. In ancient times fathers and mothers taught their children from the Scriptures, and the prester in every chamber house and the reciters in every little village read to the people from the Old Books one day in every five. But even then, that would have been a hard question to answer.

"Let me sleep on it, Jack, and ponder it all day tomorrow. And the next time we camp, I'll try to answer. I'm too tired now. I need my sleep."

He settled into his bed of leaves, closed his eyes, and was soon asleep, snoring softly.

"I can't get to sleep just yet," Jack said.

"Nor I," Ellayne said. "I do love a good story, Jack. I wonder why my father never told me any of the stories from the Old Books. Why didn't he teach me anything about God?"

"Maybe nobody ever taught him."

"He says things like, 'God only knows how much money that'll cost,' or 'Why in God's name should I do that,' but he never really talks about God. He prays when everybody else prays, on Assembly days at the chamber house—and that's all."

"What are you getting at?" Jack said.

"Well, we're going to climb Bell Mountain and ring the bell because God wants us to, and maybe when the bell rings, the whole world will come to an end—I mean, we ought to know *why*," Ellayne said.

That was more than Jack could answer because he simply didn't know why. But they'd hiked through the woods all day, and now their fire was dying down, and before too much longer, they were both asleep.

It seemed to Jack that he'd hardly drifted off when there was a loud cry that woke him up, the fire was out, the light was grey, and Obst was thrashing around beside him, scattering dead leaves and groaning. Jack tried to grab an arm and shake him, but only got clouted for his pains.

Ellayne scrambled out of the shelter. Wytt hopped around beside her, chattering, whistling, and brandishing his sharpened stick.

And Obst sat up with a groan.

"What's the matter now!" Jack said, still smarting where the back of Obst's hand had struck him across the cheek.

"Oh! Your dream, Jack—I've had your dream! It's terrible!"

He shook all over. Ellayne crawled back into the shelter and put Hesket's blanket over him. He pulled it tightly around his shoulders. Jack heard his teeth chattering.

"It was just the way you told it, child," he said, stammering. "The great voice of the bell, rolling down from the mountain, filling and shaking the whole world. Aah!"

"I had the dream, too—once," Ellayne said. "It was bad, but not that bad."

Obst ran off a long recitation of Scripture in the original language. Jack didn't understand a word of it. But it made Obst's teeth stop chattering.

"You haven't changed your mind again, have you—about helping us get to the mountain?" Ellayne asked.

He shook his head.

"No," he said. "I wouldn't dare. Let someone else defy the will of God. I'm too old to try. But I grieve for the world, that it should sink into fire as Caha sank into the sea, and be no more."

"Sink into fire?" the children cried together.

"After a protracted period of tribulation," the hermit

said. "As Prophet Ryshah said, 'Art thou mad, to wish for the day of the Lord?'"

A hot flash of anger tore through Jack's heart.

"I don't believe it!" he said. "I don't believe King Ozias put that bell up there so God could destroy the world as soon as somebody rang it and burn up all the good people with the bad! And He wouldn't need us for that."

Obst looked long and hard at him, as if Jack had just uttered a new prophecy in the ancient language of the Scriptures.

"What's wrong? What did I say that was wrong?" Jack said.

"I'm not sure," Obst said, very softly indeed. "All I know is that my fear has been removed. It's all gone—God's mercy to an old man. And maybe more than mercy. Maybe I need to listen more carefully when children speak."

CHAPTER 22

Three Guests, No Host

The lifeline of Obann was the Imperial River. Along its banks, from the mountains to the sea, the Oligarchy and the town councils saw to it that there was law and order. Ore from the mountains, lumber from the forested hills, bales of wool and sacks of grain—all found their way to market by transportation on or along the river. To keep this traffic flowing, militia patrolled, inspectors inspected, and work crews maintained the roads and docks.

Once there were roads through Lintum Forest, and taverns and hostels where the roads met, and the king's reeves to keep the peace. Once there were hunting lodges and summer pleasances for the rich, and foresters to mind the deer.

But that was before the Empire fell. Now the land was wilderness, abandoned to the likes of Bort and Tumm and their patron, Latt Squint-eye.

Martis spent a pleasant night with the two outlaws. They knew where the hermit kept hidden a clay jug that held more than water: it was a kind of berry wine he made, just the thing for keeping warm on a cool, clammy evening in a country not yet touched by spring. Bort served them only a cup of wine each, then carefully put the jug back where he'd found it.

"I see you hold this hermit in high esteem—otherwise you'd have helped yourselves to all his wine," Martis said. He took a sip and found it better than good. "How has he earned your respect? Tell me all about him. The Temple is very interested in him."

Bort sat by the fire. "We all like Obst," he said. "He's a healer, and he doesn't ask questions or take sides. His house is a safe place for anyone who visits it. All he asks is peace, so there's no fighting, no killing here. If men have a quarrel, and they end up here, they set it aside for a little while. More often than not, Obst patches it up between them. We think a lot of him for that. Makes life easier for everyone."

Humbug, Martis thought. "I can hardly wait to meet him," he said. "If I set out after him tomorrow, do you think I might catch up?"

"Ought to catch up easily, you being on horseback and him with two children to take care of."

Martis took care to reveal nothing beyond a mild curiosity about the children. But this was splendid news! His mission was all but accomplished. He'd found them. Now all he had to do was follow them up Bell Mountain and see what they found at the summit.

"Are they safe with the hermit?" he asked.

"Safe enough," Bort said. "He has a safe-conduct from Latt. But that won't stop someone from grabbing the kiddies, someone who doesn't care what Latt thinks of it. I admit there's some like that."

"Funny about that donkey, though," Tumm said.

"Donkey? What donkey?"

"Oh, the kiddies had a donkey that looked like one that belongs to a friend of ours, Hesket the Tinker," Bort said.

"Obst said it belonged to the kids. I'd say they must've stolen it from Hesket, only you couldn't steal as much as a wink from him. He's the best thief in the country. Anyhow, Obst wouldn't steal, not even from a thief."

Martis didn't tell them that their friend the thief lay dead on the plain. The children must have picked up the donkey as it wandered loose without a master.

They were prospering, he thought. They'd acquired a beast of burden and a guide. As a pupil of Lord Reesh, Martis did not attribute this to God's watchful benevolence. But there was such a thing as good luck, and it seemed these children had it.

By and by, as the fire in Obst's hearth burned down, the three men unrolled their blankets for sleep. Martis closed his eyes but kept his ears open, pretending to slumber. He could tell by the sound of him that Bort was pretending, too—although Tumm did drop off, soon enough. Martis wondered if all three of them would still be alive by the morning. He knew he would be.

As the night wore on, his thoughts wandered to the old volume of Scripture that the hermit kept on his shelf, and from there to older books that Reesh had in his private library, relics of the days of the Empire.

"There are secrets in these books, Martis," the First Prester said, when he showed them to his servant. "I've kept these secrets, and you must keep them, too. They are secrets of a glorious age—glorious days that will come again, if we do our work well."

The books contained marvels, he said: things that the world had forgotten. His eyes glowed as he spoke of them.

"Ships that traveled to the farthest isles without the need of sails. Enormous carriages propelled by fire. Weapons to demolish a city's walls in an instant.

"And things that seem impossible—miraculous! Things we haven't yet begun to understand. The ancients built devices that were capable of flight, like birds. And they knew a way to speak to one another over great distances as easily as I'm speaking to you.

"It was all lost, Martis, destroyed in the ruination of the Empire. But we can find it again, if we can unlock the secrets contained in these books."

Very, very quietly—but still making enough noise to interrupt Martis' reverie—Bort and Tumm got up and collected their blankets. Martis had his knife in his hand, but he didn't need it. Almost soundlessly, the two outlaws crept out of the cottage and retreated into the woods.

Then Martis permitted himself to sleep.

Obst said they would have to collect more food before they could move on and that this was a good part of the forest for it. He showed Jack and Ellayne where to dig for edible bulbs while he went off to set snares. "A pity you couldn't have come during berry season," he said.

He'd just gone off, and the children were poking sticks into the ground to loosen the roots, when a deep voice behind them said, "Hello! What's this?"

It was a great big man, a huge man, and they hadn't heard him coming: not a whisper of a leaf against his thighs, not the least crackle from the dead leaves on the forest floor. He stood right behind them, with a long staff in one hand and the other on his hips, tall, with wide shoulders and a barrel chest. He wore clothes that seemed to be made of nothing but patches, and no two of them the same color. His fair hair was a thicket, complete with burrs and bits of leaf.

"Who are you, and what are you doing in my woods?" he said. "Speak up!" And he shook his staff at them.

Jack's tongue froze. Obst had told them not to speak to anyone they met. But where was Obst?

"Please, sir—we're looking for the Seven Hags," Ellayne said. "Have you seen them?"

The huge man stared at her for a second, then threw back his head and laughed. He sounded like two houses being banged together.

"Oh! You mean *those* Seven Hags!" he said. "Why, they've all gone off with Abombalbap. Gone off to visit the Chief Giant in his castle!"

He was more frightening when he laughed, Jack thought. What sane man would laugh so loud? And if he wasn't the chief giant of these parts, who was?

"Burn me if I don't know a princess when I see one, even when she travels in disguise," he said, when at last he'd stopped guffawing. "Quick, now, princess—where do you come from, and what's your business with the Seven Hags?"

Before Ellayne could answer, his face suddenly went grim and he spun around as fast as lightning. His staff made a terrifying *swoosh*! as it clove the air.

It missed Obst's skull by a finger's width.

"Ha!" he cried. "That was pretty good sneaking, Obst, but not good enough. I had you pegged, old man—just waiting for you to come closer."

"Almost too close, Helki," said the hermit.

"No—I knew it was you all along," the huge man said. "I've been watching you all morning. Never knew I was here, did you? Admit it!"

"Not until you laughed. There's no one who can touch you for woodcraft, and that's the truth. But I hope you haven't terrified these children."

"Me—frighten children? Don't be daft. I was just having a little fun with 'em. They'll tell you so themselves."

Obst came up and clapped the big man's shoulder. "Children, this is Helki—Helki the Rod, we call him. He looks ferocious, but he wouldn't hurt you. He's not even an outlaw."

"He knows about the Seven Hags," Ellayne said. "I thought they were only in my storybook."

"I don't know about books," said Helki, "but Lintum Forest is full of stories, and I reckon I know burnt-near all of 'em. They're part of the place, like the trees. I can show you the spot where King Ozias was born and a great hole in the ground that used to be the castle where the Enchantress kept Abombalbap prisoner for a year and a day.

"But even better, I can show you the carcass of a buck I killed just yesterday, and Obst won't have to bother to set snares if you want to eat. That is, if you'd like to visit my camp. It's not far."

Helki led them to his camp, moving silently through narrow places along the path where the children and their donkey made a noisy thrashing. He didn't hurry, but his strides were so long that even Obst had to hustle to keep up. In half an hour they were at a clearing where a deer hung on a makeshift tripod to be cleaned and a lean-to stood over a bed of green ferns. A pile of firewood lay beside a circle of blackened stones.

"Sit down. Start a fire if you'd like a cup of tea. I'll cut some venison for you," Helki said. "And then, Obst, you can tell me who these children are and what you're doing with them."

There were logs to sit on. Obst got the fire going. He brewed some tea that Helki had in his pack. "Good stuff," Helki said, "from beyond the mountains and away down south." It had an aroma that made Jack think of apple blossoms, and a flavor that he couldn't place. "Almonds," Helki said; but Jack didn't know what almonds were.

Helki stood a log on end and sat on it. "Well," he said, "tell me your tale."

"I'd rather not," Obst said, "except to say that what I'm doing, I do in God's service. You understand."

The giant nodded. "I reckon I do. All right, so be it. But I'll tell you one thing. You'll have to cut the girl's hair a bit closer if you want anyone to take her for a boy."

"I cut it," Jack said.

"You're no barber, then, my lad," Helki said. Jack looked up at his wild thicket of hair, with the burrs caught in it, and wondered what he knew of barbers.

The aroma of the tea lured Wytt out of hiding. He hopped up to Ellayne and sniffed the steam coming from her cup, then looked up at Helki and chittered at him.

Helki chittered back, and whistled; and Wytt answered him; and they went back and forth while Jack and Ellayne stared at them, astonished.

"Are you talking to him?" Ellayne cried.

"You can't rightly call it talk—not like people talk,"

Helki said. "But it's more than any animal can do. In his way, he was telling me that he's your friend, and I'd better be nice to you or I'll have to answer to him; and I told him I'm your friend, too, just like he is."

"But how did you learn to talk to Omahs?" Jack said.

"There's a great heap of ruins south of the forest. I go there sometimes. There's a tribe of these little hairy people living there. I made friends with 'em years ago. If you're careful about listening, you learn to understand 'em by and by."

He shook his head. Jack noticed, for the first time, that Helki's eyes weren't quite the same color: two different shades of green.

"You do see some funny things when you're up in the ruins," he said. "Makes you wonder what those places used to be and what happened there. But the little people can't tell you. They don't know."

Helki fed them with fresh venison, roasted over the fire, and gave them some rabbits to take with them.

"I ought to go with you. I can protect you," he said. "I've been seeing queer animals lately. There's a striped beast with jaws that would snap a man in two with one bite."

"We saw it!" Jack said. "It was carrying half of a knuckle-bear in its mouth. What is it?"

"Wish I knew," Helki said. "I've seen some tracks, too, that don't match up with anything I know. Maybe they're coming over the mountains. Or maybe they're just coming up out of the ground.

"But beasts are only beasts. It's men you ought to fear. There's those hereabouts who'd be better off for a taste of this." And he balanced his heavy staff on a fingertip.

"I have a safe-conduct from Squint-eye," Obst said.

"I wouldn't trust to that."

"If you want to help us, Helki, I'd be thankful if you stayed in this region of the forest and kept your eyes and ears open. Try to discover where the beasts are coming from. Keep track of unusual things. That's what I'd be doing, if I could. I can't ask anyone else to do it. They don't understand the forest like you do. Their eyes don't see; their ears don't hear. You understand."

"Reckon I do."

Obst reached out and squeezed his arm. "And for the Lord's sake, stay alive!" he said. "Stop looking for trouble."

Helki threw back his head and laughed like thunder.

After they had hiked some distance, Ellayne asked the hermit, "Why didn't you want him to come with us? He's strong!"

"He's also as mad as a bat," Obst said. "If he were with us, everyone else in the forest would know it, and he'd want to fight with every one of them."

"With that big stick?" Jack said.

"It's all he needs. But someday someone will put an arrow in his back, or poison him, or fifty men will overwhelm him—if Helki doesn't kill Latt first."

They walked on. Another day, Obst said, and they'd turn aside, leave the forest, and make for the hills.

CHAPTER 23

Strange Beasts in the Land

Coming out of the forest and onto the plains again and seeing the mountains from a new angle, it struck Jack for the first time that a mountain was a formidable thing, and it might not like to be climbed.

Up rose Bell Mountain with its crown of clouds, Mount Nevereen huddled up against it, and various sharp, snow-capped crags standing like a bodyguard around it. How could they hope to climb up to the clouds? From this unfamiliar angle, the peaks looked like a hostile army pausing to take one last look at a doomed city before destroying it. Jack could almost believe the mountains were watching them as they toiled along like insects, just waiting for them to get close enough to be crushed.

"Had we gone all the way to Silvertown," Obst was saying, "we would have found trails to take us along the skirts of the mountains, practically up to the shoulders of Bell Mountain itself. There are mines and lumber camps scattered throughout the hills, but all paths lead to Silvertown.

"Instead, we'll cross the plain and go slowly up and up to the forests that cover the foothills; and then for most of the way we'll have to find our own paths, or even make them. When we come out of those woods, we'll be on the slopes of Bell Mountain. God help us."

"My teacher back home said anyone would get killed who tried to climb the mountain," Jack said. "He said you'd fall off, or freeze to death, or be crushed by falling rocks."

"And there are evil spirits on some mountains," Ellayne put in. "They can bring fog and make you get lost, and they come at night and drink your blood while you sleep."

Obst threw a stern look at her. "If God has called you to the top of the mountain, He'll see that you get there. But there's danger enough in the world without a need for evil spirits. That's just a lot of Heathen superstition."

"Well, it was in my storybook," Ellayne said.

Obst made no answer, but led them tirelessly across the plain, making for the green-clad hills in the far distance to the north and east.

"Do we have to go so fast?" Jack said.

"I'm always happier under cover of the trees," Obst said. "It's safer."

"What can happen to us out here?"

"Enough. Slave-traders, robbers—and maybe beasts."

"Please, Obst—where do the beasts come from?" Ellayne said. "Like the knuckle-bears and that horrible striped thing we saw in the woods. Do the Old Books have anything to say about them?"

They went on for another hundred yards before Obst began to answer.

"When the Children of Geb first set foot upon the mainland and history began," he said, "there were many kinds of beasts that had to be subdued before the people could live in the land. Some we still have with us—the wolf and the bear, the wildcat and the catamount, and the wild boar. Others are no longer seen in Obann, but still inhabit other countries—the lion and the leopard, the wild dog, and the rhinoceros. And some are not to be found anywhere, unless it be far to the south or far to the north where no man ever goes. But men remember them—the dragon and the basilisk, the satyr and the gryphon, and the cockatrice with poison hotter than an adder's.

"But there were still other beasts. Of some, nothing remains but an old name in an ancient language, a word that has no meaning anymore. We see these words in Scripture, but there are no descriptions to go with them. Mumheer, allabach, vehoma, kecharr—those are some of the names. And there were beasts whose names are not recorded.

"I have come to believe that God is bringing back those beasts that were lost. You've seen some of them, and I've seen more. To what end, who can say? Maybe to devour a wicked and rebellious people from off the face of the earth."

Jack thought about that for some minutes, but Ellayne spoke first.

"But you said the knuckle-bears were harmless," she said. "And Jack shot with his slingshot a little hoppy animal with big ears and a long nose, and we ate it for supper. Beasts like those wouldn't devour anybody."

"Do the Old Books say that God will bring back the beasts to kill off the people?" Jack asked.

Obst stopped walking, and suddenly grinned at him.

"My boy, you have the makings of a theologian!" he said. "No, the Scriptures say no such thing, neither in the Prophets nor the Songs. So I'd be wise to dismiss the thought! I don't know why there are strange beasts in the land these days. I simply don't know!"

But it was Martis who had the most perilous encounter with a beast, and this is how it happened.

Having been told by outlaws that Obst was going to Silvertown, but knowing that the children's true goal was Bell Mountain, Martis wanted to catch up to them and follow closely. He doubted they'd go all the way to Silvertown: that was almost as far from the mountain as Ninneburky. It was the chief of all the mining towns; and if I were minding children, he thought, I certainly wouldn't take them there. Every slaver and kidnapper in Obann passed through Silvertown. He was sure the hermit knew that, and had simply lied to Bort and Tumm.

Martis reasoned that the hermit would lead the children out of the forest on a course for Bell Mountain. If he knew the lay of the land as Martis knew it from maps, he would want to cross the plain where the forests of the foothills reached farthest south and west. It was on the plains that they'd be most vulnerable to human predators; the hermit would want to cross as quickly as possible.

Martis decided to travel along the fringe of the forest, where he could watch the plains. He could question anyone he met: an old man accompanied by two children would be conspicuous. He found a northerly trail and spurred his horse to a trot, expecting to break out of the forest by midday. What he didn't expect was for his horse to fight him, shuddering under the saddle.

"What ails you, cousin?" he said, fighting for control with reins and spurs.

Right beside him, a wall of underbrush and saplings burst open with a roar, and Martis was unhorsed, hurled backward onto the trail. And the horse screamed.

But not for long. With a loud crack, a massive beak crushed the horse's neck and cut off its scream. The beak belonged to a creature spawned in a madman's fevered nightmare—a gigantic bird that had to bend down to seize a horse's neck. Legs like scaly pillars, useless tiny wings that flapped excitedly, matted grey feathers shot with white and blue, a long powerful neck, staring yellow eyes as big as teacups, and a hooked beak as mighty as a pair of clashing millstones: that was what Martis saw. Before he could catch his breath, it killed his horse.

It shook once, then dropped the limp and lifeless body to the forest floor.

Then it spotted Martis.

At first he couldn't move a muscle. The yellow eyes glared at him. He'd never seen or heard of such a thing in all his life. What could a man do against such a monster? A bird that might weigh as much as a big bear!

It glared at him, then opened that vast beak and cawed.

Martis scrambled backward into the foliage, somehow found his feet, and fled in a blind panic. He didn't stop until he ran right into a fallen log and fell over it, landing face-first in a mire of wet, sticky, rotting leaves.

Only then did he realize that the bird had not pursued him. Why should it, when it had his horse to eat?

He rose to his knees, turned and looked back, clinging to the creeper-covered trunk of the fallen tree. It had been a very long time since Martis had experienced pure, overpowering fear. Now it drained out of him, leaving him exhausted but rational.

I'll need my pack! he thought. My tinderbox, my map, my money, my credentials—I've got to get them back. He would have to wait until the bird had eaten its fill and moved on.

When he felt strong enough, he got up and crept back the way he'd come. Broken bushes and gouges in the leaf-litter marked his trail like signposts. It was not as long a trail as he thought. He stopped when he heard the bird ripping flesh from bone and noisily gulping it down: stopped and hid behind a stout oak tree until the noise stopped.

After what he deemed a long enough wait, he crept a little closer, silently. He peered through a screen of brush. The great bird was gone.

It had eaten half his horse, tossing the head aside, gobbling up the neck—bones and all—and tearing the meat and hide off the rest of the carcass. It must have devoured several hundred pounds of flesh in a few minutes.

Martis found his pack a few yards from the horse. Now he had everything he needed—except a weapon with which he could hope to defend himself, should he meet the bird again. It wouldn't leave much of a man's body uneaten. But then what weapon would avail against a creature that attacked from ambush?

He shouldered his pack, wrapped the leather thong of his mace around his wrist, and marched. The mire he'd fallen into stained his clothes, his hands, and his face, and it stank. Maybe it would protect him from beasts that hunted by scent.

By noontime he was out of the thick of the forest, in sight of the plains, and hot and winded from the hard pace he'd set himself. He rested against a tree, embracing the trunk, and then began to tremble all over from head to toe, and couldn't stop.

A bit later Helki came upon what was left of Martis' horse, and marveled. He'd never seen the giant bird, but he'd seen its tracks before, and he saw them again, here.

"Look at that!" he said to himself. "Well, where there's a horse, there's a man. Let's see what's left of the rider."

He read the marks: man thrown clear of horse, bolts into underbrush, and then returns, has a look-round, and resumes his journey. That didn't sound like any man Helki knew. An outlaw would've fled back the way he'd come, and wouldn't have come back.

Helki decided to follow him: he wanted to meet that man. If nothing else, the rider could describe the creature that had killed his horse.

CHAPTER 24

What Jack Saw by Starlight

Latt Squint-eye insisted on dues being paid to him by every man in his part of Lintum Forest, but there was one thing he valued even more: news. For that reason, Bort interrupted his dues-collecting to hurry back to Squint-eye's camp with his news.

The self-styled King of the Forest might have been a beautiful baby once, but now he was a hideous man. His left eye squinted. His right eye goggled, and around it was tattooed a blue serpent that writhed when he spoke. A ghastly white scar ran diagonally across his forehead; but the man who'd given him that was dead. He missed a few teeth, and the one eyetooth that remained on the right side of his jaw, he'd filed to a sharp point. He braided his grey hair and beard into many braids, and sometimes stuck slow-burning fuses into his beard to accentuate an already daunting appearance. But of course the most daunting thing about him was that he'd murdered a great many men to gain his position, and was willing to murder many more to keep it.

"So!" he growled, when he'd heard Bort's news. "The Temple sends out a real killer, all this way from Obann, just to visit a harmless balmy hermit. And they think I'm fool enough to believe it!

"You've never lived in the City, Bort; you don't know the presters like I know them. Holy men—bah! They're worse thieves that we could ever be. Like as not they've found out there's money to be made in Lintum Forest, provided they stretch a few necks first, beginning with mine and yours. Then the free men can pay their dues to the Temple instead of to the likes of us.

"Well, I'll tell you what to do. Take ten men and find that popinjay from the Temple, and bring him back to me. Able to talk, mind you! I've got a few questions I'd like to ask him. And then we'll see whose neck gets stretched."

Bort lost no time in choosing nine of the most accomplished manslayers in the camp, including two or three adept at tracking and leading them in pursuit of the killer from the Temple.

Martis hiked eastward along the fringe of the forest, pushing himself at a brisk pace. He felt exposed and vulnerable without his horse—absurd, he chided himself, considering what had happened to the horse. But he was not used to being afraid, and the fear had worked itself down into a deep place in his soul where he couldn't fight it.

He discovered now that he'd been inwardly sneering at his patron, Lord Reesh, for being afraid of a dream. Reesh, of all men, giving in to religious superstition! Martis had always admired his master's ability to rule the Temple without believing in any of the medieval mummery it stood for. For a little thing like a dream to shake his unbelief was unworthy of him. But now that he himself was shaken, Martis sympathized with his master.

It'll pass, he promised himself. I'll carry on with the mission; I'll follow those moonstruck children up the mountain—if they get there!—and see nothing happen when they ring the bell, if there is a bell. And by the time it's all over, I'll be myself again.

It's all tripe and superstition, he told himself. A lot of foolishness left over from ancient times, cobwebs and all. Even if some fanatic, thousands of years ago, had managed to erect a bell atop Mount Yul, and the bell were still there today, you could ring it until your arms fell off and nothing would come of it. God wouldn't hear it because there is no God. The ancients believed in God, and where were they? It was all superstition—albeit useful superstition, because the Temple was a device to hold the nation together. By all that was reasonable and sane, the God of the Scriptures would have blasted the Temple ten times over if He knew but half of what the Temple did in His name! Including any number of assassinations performed by Martis himself in the service of the Temple.

By such arguments, and by pushing himself as hard as his legs would tolerate, Martis came near to calming himself. But from time to time the vision of that terrible bird crushing the horse's neck in its beak rushed back to him and made him shiver, and wrung his stomach into a knot, and oppressed his heart.

"There are no birds like that!" he would mutter to himself. "It was a thing that should not be!"

But the fact that he was walking now, instead of riding, argued otherwise.

Helki took his time following the stranger's trail, which for him was as easy to read as a page in a book would be for you. It told him that the man was hurrying along as if a pack of wolves were baying at his heels. The man stumbled frequently, but never fell: mighty determined to get to wherever he's going, Helki thought.

Sooner or later the man would have to stop. Helki didn't hurry. The stranger would stop when he'd used up all his strength, and then it would take him some time to get going again. Helki would catch up to him before then.

Obst had never traveled from Lintum Forest to the wooded foothills, and he'd underestimated the distance. Late afternoon found him and the children still on the plains, with maybe another full day's hard marching to go before they reached the hills.

"It's time we chose a spot to camp for the night," he said. "I'd rather not spend a night out here, but there's no help for it. Just pray our fire doesn't attract slavers."

"We don't know how to pray without a prester," Ellayne said. "We did try it once, but I'm sure we didn't do it right."

Obst smiled at her. "It's very hard to do it wrong, child," he said. "Just set your mind on God and talk to Him, aloud or silently. He'll hear you."

"How can He hear us if we do it silently?" Jack said. He'd never heard of such a thing.

"The Most High Lord who created you knows you better than you know yourself," Obst said. "He knows every thought you've ever had. He's not a man, who must live in the world and depend on his eyes and ears. You can be sure

He'll hear you when you pray."

Jack put an arm around the donkey's shoulder and leaned on him a little, resting. Ham nuzzled him.

"Why didn't the prester ever tell us that?" he asked.

"You'd have to ask him. Come, we'd better make camp. It'll be dark soon."

It wasn't much of a camp, just a few bushes between them and the cold wind blowing down from the mountains, and as big a fire as they could manage. Obst had them cut clumps of gorse and lace them into the branches of the bushes that sheltered them, the better to block the wind.

Somehow Obst and Ellayne were able to fall asleep right away after they ate; and Wytt cuddled up in Ellayne's arms and occasionally made faint meeping noises in his sleep, as if he were dreaming hard. Jack wondered what Omahs dreamed. He couldn't fall asleep, as tired as he was. He kept wondering why, if God could hear silent prayers, anyone would need to attract His attention with a bell. If he tried to discuss such a thing with his stepfather, Van would have him declared mad and send him away.

Jack decided to get up and see what Bell Mountain looked like by starlight. None of his companions stirred as he crawled out from his blanket and crept past the dying campfire. Ham, tethered to a stake in the ground, nickered at him. He stood beside the donkey and petted him.

"Look at them, Ham," he whispered, meaning the mountains. "Do you think we'll ever get there, really? They don't look any closer than they did when we started out."

But the sight of the starlight on the mountain snows was worth getting up for. By night Bell Mountain's crown of clouds had a mysterious silvery glow. Jack wondered what lay hidden in those clouds. He wondered if God could see through the clouds.

Ham suddenly shuddered and went stiff—ears up, nostrils quivering, eyes rolling. Jack clasped his arms around his neck to keep him from bolting, and tried to see what Ham saw.

There—about as far as Jack could throw a stone: taller than the tallest man, taller than a horse, with a head bigger than a horse's head—a colossal bird stood looking at him, with one of its enormous legs bent as if it were poised to charge. It carried itself just like one of the little white egrets you saw wading in the quiet shallows of a pond, dark against the starlit plain, as massive as a tree. There was nothing like it in all the world. And it was close, much too close. With those two long legs, it would quickly run down anyone who tried to escape.

But Jack wasn't running; his feet froze to the earth. Ham was frozen, too.

The bird shook a pair of ridiculously undersized wings, and Jack could hear its feathers rattle. It shook its wings twice, turned its head, and then stalked off. Its great hooked beak pointed the way, and its heavy head on its ess-shaped neck bobbed back and forth as it went. Jack glimpsed at great clawed feet. It just walked off, and Jack watched until it vanished into the night.

His breath came back with a whoosh. He was terrified that Ham would make a noise and call the monster back, but the donkey only blew hard and shook its ears and shivered. Jack would have fallen if he hadn't been holding on to

Ham's neck.

It was gone. It could have run right up and killed us, Jack thought, and it just walked away. He couldn't understand it.

The wind blew, chilling him. He shivered. He kissed the donkey good night and crept back to the others, wrapping himself tightly in his blanket and wedging himself between Ellayne and Obst because he was so cold. Wytt whimpered and stirred in Ellayne's arms, but didn't wake.

For some reason Jack didn't want to wake the others. He didn't want to talk, not with his teeth chattering. And while he was trying to decide what to say, he fell into a deep and dreamless sleep.

CHAPTER 25

The Rod Strikes

Toward the end of the afternoon, the man Helki was tracking went slower and slower. Helki knew the man would soon have to stop, and knew he was catching up to him. But if you'd been there to watch Helki, you wouldn't have seen him.

As closely as he studied the stranger's trail, Helki paid just as much attention to everything else around him. He noticed when the birds stopped calling to proclaim their territory or attract mates for the nesting season, which would soon begin; now they called out warnings. One jay was louder and angrier than all the other birds. Helki paid special heed to its cawings.

Someone or something was on the move, coming closer by the moment, and the birds didn't like it. Soon squirrels were chattering about it, too.

So Helki melted into the shadows among the trees and blended into the undergrowth. The birds ignored him. It may have been that they could neither see nor hear him.

Now he followed the noise instead of tracks. Maybe he would meet the unknown animal that had killed the stranger's horse. But as he paused from time to time to sniff the breeze, it brought him the scent of unwashed men who'd worked up a new sweat. There were quite a few of them. Before long Helki could hear them crashing through the underbrush and the faint sound of their voices.

Helki kept a safe distance from them, stalking them by sound and scent. He knew they must be some of Latt's men and guessed they were chasing the same stranger that he'd been following all afternoon. One of their lookouts must have seen the man and told them where to find him.

Helki smiled to himself. They were so hot to rob the stranger that they took no thought to the possibility of themselves being robbed.

He let them get a little farther ahead, but not out of earshot. They blundered along the narrow paths, cursing when they got caught on brambles. But Helki didn't need a path. There were great elk in Lintum Forest, huge creatures that could pass through a dense thicket without so much as a rustle. Helki learned how to move through the forest by studying them.

As he neared the edge of the woods, he heard loud voices. He slowed his approach. The trees here wouldn't have been close enough together to hide a smaller man, but they hid Helki. Soon he could see Latt's men, but they couldn't see him.

But they wouldn't have. It was getting dark, and they were busy with their prey.

Having gone as far as he could go, Martis had stopped to gather firewood and make a camp while he still had some strength left for it. He was sure he'd want a cuss't big fire burning all night. If there were monster birds hunting by day, there was no telling what would come out at night.

Why had he never heard of gigantic birds in Lintum Forest? There were many fabulous beasts mentioned in the Old Books, but not those. There were idle romances, children's fairy tales, and silly songs that told of unipeds, men who walked backwards because their faces were on the wrong side of their heads, and giants, centaurs, and hobgoblins—but there was nothing in any of them about horrible birds that ate horses. What did it mean, that there were now such things in Lintum Forest?

Martis stacked a high pile of firewood, enough to last all night. Exhausted, he supposed he'd better start the fire right away. Luckily he hadn't lost his tinderbox, and he still had his water bottle and a few bites to eat. It was only jerky, wayfarers' food; but he was too tired to long for braised lamb and wine. And it would soon be dark.

If he hadn't been so weary and so preoccupied with starting his fire, he might have heard something that would have made him prepare to defend himself. But he heard nothing at all until a band of men burst out of the woods and surrounded him.

"Don't try to fight, elder brother! You're one man against ten."

It was with something akin to relief that Martis recognized the fat outlaw with whom he'd passed the night at the hermit's house. He held up his empty palms in surrender.

"If you've come to rob me, Bort, you've come too late," he said. "I've lost my horse. A giant bird killed it and ate it."

"What happened to your horse?"

"A bird ate it. A bird that's bigger than a horse. You live here. You must have seen it sometime."

One of Bort's men looked at his leader quizzically. "What's he saying, Bort? What's this about a giant bird?"

"Never mind, Skrup. Elder brother, we've come for you,

not your horse. You're our prisoner. Our chief, Latt Squint-eye, wants to meet you. So let's see your weapons. Hand 'em over. Then we can sit down and talk about birds. It's too late now to head back to camp."

Martis surrendered his mace and a rather expensive little dagger he wore in his belt. His skewer he left in his lapel: they might not notice it, and he might get a chance to use it later. They didn't notice, but Bort had two men tie his wrists together with a strip of hide. Only then did the outlaws sit down around the fire.

"Now we're all comfortable," Bort said. "Now you can tell us about your bird."

Martis told him. He was amazed they knew nothing of it. But the way some of them cast uneasy glances at the dark woods told him they believed him.

"There've been some queer beasts around lately, that's for certain," Bort said. "Don't ask me where they came from. Twenty years I've lived in these parts and never seen the like of it until a year ago. But what I'm interested in is your reason for being here, elder brother. It's a long way from Obann."

"I told you," Martis said. "I came to meet the hermit. The Temple is interested in him. There are stories that he performs miracles."

Bort leaned closer to him. "If you try to tell Latt that story, he'll burn your eyes out."

"It's the truth. What other reason could I possibly have for being in a place like this?"

"Whatever it is, you'll tell it before Latt's done with you," the outlaw said. "The Temple's always looking for more money, says Latt. Maybe the Temple would like to get its paws on Lintum Forest—eh? There's trade with the Heathen over the mountains and gold going back and forth. Gold that might wind up in the Temple's treasury, if men like us were put out of the way."

"There's much more money in miracles."

Bort smashed Martis' cheek with the back of his hand, knocking him onto his back, rousing a laugh from the men. Stunned, Martis offered no resistance when Bort pulled him back up by the hair. The pain was like a fire in his scalp.

"You'd have killed me and Tumm if we'd given you the chance, that night in the cabin," Bort said. "A man like you doesn't come all the way out here to chase after moonshine."

Martis looked him in the eye. "A man like me will be the death of you, fat boy. The Temple will see to that."

Bort's fist crashed into his nose. Martis fell again. This time Bort let him lie there. Overhead, the stars were coming out. Martis felt blood seeping thickly from his nose.

"Better save some of that for Latt, fat boy," one of the men said. The others laughed.

This was going to be bad, Martis thought. Because the Temple alone collected tax in every part of the country, it was the only apparatus of the government that had enemies everywhere. Some of these hated the Temple out of all proportion to the offense. Martis had encountered it many times before. Temple-hating was a passion, for which the tax was only an excuse.

"They hate us because they crave from us more than we can give them," Lord Reesh often said. "They hunger for God, and we can't give them God. We give them a reason to think of themselves as a nation and some hope of there maybe being something better than this life in this world. If they understood their own desire, they would hate us even more. Let us be thankful that they don't understand."

Reesh was right. It's why the hermit has nothing to fear from these ferocious men, Martis thought—but I do.

"Get up, you. I'm talking to you," Bort said. This time he pulled Martis up by the front of his shirt.

And then something happened.

Some deep voice roared, "The rod! The rod!" It was like a bull's bellow. All the outlaws went into a panic, and Bort let go of Martis' shirt and scrambled to his feet.

Everyone was moving, yelling. A man went down like a sack of grain and lay still. By firelight all Martis could see was that the camp was under attack. Another gang of outlaws? A man screamed and stumbled past, almost into the fire, clutching at an injured arm. Martis saw Bort scuttle into the forest, followed by others. Taken totally by surprise, they didn't even try to resist. They only fled the scene, and it didn't take them long to do it.

Besides Martis himself, there was only one man left—a giant of a man who stood erect with his powerful shoulders thrown back, breathing like a blacksmith's bellows, with a staff in one hand planted on the ground like a conquering army's standard. He faced the woods. Martis heard the outlaws thrashing in the undergrowth as they fled.

"Come back any time you please!" the giant roared. "Tell your chief that Helki the Rod has beaten you—Helki the Rod! Ha, ha!"

What lunatic was this, who single-handedly attacked ten men and routed them like mice? He stood on guard, still breathing hard, until the noise of the bandits' retreat diminished into silence.

"They won't be coming back—more's the pity," he said. He turned, and squatted on his heels in front of Martis. He wore a fantastic garment of patches and a wild mane of hair.

"It's too bad they roughed you up, stranger. But it could've been worse," he said. "Hold out your hands, I'll cut you loose."

Martis obeyed. He pulled a short-bladed knife from one of his boots and cut the hide thongs in one easy motion.

"Who are you?" Martis said.

"I found your horse and followed your trail. I wanted to ask you what happened to that horse and find out your business. We don't see many strangers around here. My name's Helki. This forest is my home. Latt's pack can't drive me out."

"Thank you for rescuing me. I thought you were another gang."

Helki snorted. "They're cowardly scum," he said. "The forest would be better off without 'em. Why don't you have a drink of water, wash the blood off your face? Then you can tell me who you are and what you're doing here. But first tell me about the horse."

While Martis washed, Helki picked up the dead man by the belt and tossed the body into the darkness under the trees; but he kept the dead man's pack. He settled down by the fire and listened intently as Martis described his encounter with the bird.

"I've seen its tracks," he said, "so I knew it must be something like that. Though where it came from, I don't know. I haven't seen it yet. Now I reckon I will, soon enough."

Martis told him he was from the Temple at Obann,

sent to inquire into reports of a hermit who performed miracles. Helki threw back his head and guffawed. His laughter echoed among the trees.

"Haw! Who told you Obst does miracles? Unless you want to say it's a miracle no wolf or bear has eaten him, the way he goes off woolgathering. He says God protects him, and it must be true. But what do you want with him? He's a friend of mine."

"We only want to know if the miracle stories are true," Martis said. "After all, a man who can work miracles deserves to be honored."

"I don't think Obst cares about being honored."

Bort's men had left two packs behind. Helki opened them now. "There's some nice black bread here," he said. "I wonder who they stole it from. Want some?"

In spite of everything, Martis found he was hungry. When he chewed the tough, rich bread, he was relieved to discover he had no broken teeth.

Eating gave him time to think about what to say. He didn't want to make the giant suspicious of him. Helki struck him as a man who could be stabbed to the heart while he slept, and still be able to leap up and strangle his murderer before his heart stopped beating. He'd surprised the ten bandits, but Martis didn't think the ten could have stood against him even if they'd had fair warning. Martis had a trained eye for such things.

When they resumed their talk, Martis said, "I mean the hermit no harm. Men like him, if they turn out to be the real thing, make it easier for people to believe in God. It gives them hope. That's why the Temple sent me to find him. We want to know what makes him holy."

"Sounds like a lot of foolishness to me," Helki said. "Bort wouldn't have punched you around just for saying that."

"He seemed to think the Temple was plotting to take over the dues paid to outlaws."

"He also seemed to think you're a pretty dangerous man."

"I think you'll agree that this has been a pretty dangerous trip for me," Martis said. "I was chosen because my master had some hope I'd survive."

"You might—if you turn around and go back to where you came from. You might as well. Obst has gone away. We won't be seeing him for a while."

"Yes, I'd already heard that. I was hoping to catch up to him."

Helki fished for another piece of bread. He talked while he was chewing it, but Martis understood him well enough.

"If you stay around here, Latt's boys will catch up to you. They might even try to catch up to me. They'll kill you if they catch you, and they'll take their time about it, too.

"Obst asked me to stay here and look after things while he went on with those two kids. You know about them?" Martis nodded. "He didn't tell me where they're going. If I'd gone with them, you'd probably be dead by this time tomorrow. So I reckon I'd better stay here like I promised, in case anything else happens. But you—either go home or head for the mountains. That's where I think Obst is going. You'd better cross the plain as soon as you can walk. Maybe God will protect you, too."

"Do you believe in God?" Martis asked—just because he wished to know.

The giant nodded. "Obst taught me to believe."

"So you believe because he taught you?" Reesh would be interested in this, if Martis ever returned to Obann to tell him about it.

Helki grinned. "Ask me about the forest. I can't answer questions about God. Don't know how. But if you can walk, I'd start out tonight if I was you. If you get a good head start on them, they won't know how to track you across open country."

"I'd feel safer if you came with me," Martis said. "I have money. I can pay you."

"Not me," Helki said. "Tomorrow I'll start looking for the giant bird that ate your horse. That's something I want to see."

CHAPTER 26

Ellayne Discovers the Rest of the World

Ellayne found it hard to believe Jack had seen a giant bird in the night while she and Obst were sleeping. But she had to believe it when he found some of the bird's tracks in a bare patch where the ground was muddy. The bird's feet were a great deal bigger than her own, but they made the same kind of tracks that ordinary little birds make in the snow.

"I've never seen this creature," Obst said. "It must be taller than a man! All the more reason for us to get off the plain as fast as we can."

He set them a hard pace for that day's traveling. The forested hills were closer now; you'd almost think you could reach out and touch them. Although you couldn't say by how much the land was sloping generally upward, Ellayne felt it in her legs. When you turned and looked back, you could see how much higher you were than Lintum Forest in the south.

Jack and Ellayne soon had to open their coats. "It's getting warm," Jack said. "I think this must be the warmest day we've had since we started."

"Spring's late this year, but it's here at last," Obst said. "Very soon now, everything that's grey and yellow on this plain will turn bright green, and you'll see flowers in every color you can think of. See, the trees are in bud. They look red, or greenish, from a distance—not grey. The new leaves will be out before we get to Bell Mountain. And any night now we ought to hear frogs and toads calling from the little pools where the underground water seeps to the surface. Indeed, it's been spring for at least two weeks."

"My father says the weather's getting colder every year," Ellayne said.

"That's been true for the past seven years," Obst said. "I have wondered what it means, but God has hidden it from me. Yet the land has by no means become less fruitful. If anything, it's more so. You should have seen the blueberries last year! And wait until you taste the wild apples. They get sweeter every year. It's all a puzzle to me."

They hiked on and on. Wytt hopped onto the donkey and rode, clinging to the baggage. Ham rolled his eyes and twitched his ears, but after a few minutes learned to ignore his passenger.

As hard as they pushed themselves, day's end still found them short of the tree-clad hills and obliged to make camp in the open.

"We have enough food left for our supper tonight and a good breakfast tomorrow. After that, we'll have to find some more," Obst said.

He found them a hollow to camp in, protected by a screen of heather. Wytt speared a big beetle for his dinner. He toasted it over the fire, and Ellayne shut her eyes while he ate it, but couldn't shut out the crunching sounds. Jack thought that was funny.

"It doesn't look like there's much food to be found out here," she said.

"We'll find enough," Obst said. "It's all a matter of knowing where to look for it. There are always edible bulbs, birds' eggs and the birds themselves, and plump little animals to be flushed out of hiding. We won't go hungry."

After their meal he told them how the Temple was first built by the Great King, Kai, to be the center of his kingdom and draw all the people there to worship God on holy days, and how the Lord's prophet, Akan, warned him that unless the people maintained a righteous spirit, the Temple would someday become a barrier between them and their God.

"The Temple has never been what righteous Kai intended it to be," the hermit said (and at about this time, toads began to sing nearby—to Ellayne's delight). "Two hundred years later, the Heathen burned it to the ground when hordes of them came over the mountains; for the people of Obann had turned away from God and sought only their own pleasures. And they worshipped idols that their merchants brought home from the islands.

"After this they repented, and the Lord drove out the Heathen, and King Aban-sor rebuilt the Temple and made it grander than it was. But in those days when the kingdom finally came to an end and the rebellious nation drove King Ozias from his throne, there were insurrections and wars among the clans; and this time the people of Obann themselves threw down the Temple. It wasn't built again until a thousand years passed, and the Empire rose and fell.

"It is written that this last and greatest Temple, too, shall be destroyed and shall not be built again until the Lord

Himself shall build it, to stand forever."

He fell silent. Ellayne listened to the music of the toads, but Jack was quick with a question, getting it out before Obst could fall into one of his spells.

"I don't understand!" Jack said. "If God's going to make the world come to an end, where will He put the new Temple?"

Obst smiled, but not happily. "I believe He will first create a new world," he said. Jack shook his head, but Obst sank down into a sleep.

Soon Jack was asleep, too; but not Ellayne.

How could the Temple possibly be something that kept people away from God? She wondered and wondered about it. The Temple was all the people had. How many people could go out and be holy hermits like Obst? It was all very well for him to study the Scriptures. But when he recited verses from the Old Books, the language didn't make a lick of sense to her. What good would it do to read the Scriptures if you couldn't understand the language? So if they didn't have the Temple, and the chamber houses, and the presters to lead the prayers, and the reciters to give advice and teach school, the people would have had nothing at all. She knew what her father would say about that: he'd say Obst was crazy.

Unable to sleep, Ellayne got up to see if she could find the toads. There had to be one of those little pools nearby, and she wanted to see it. She'd always loved the little brown and grey toads that turned up in her mother's kitchen garden.

She tried to locate them by the sound of their singing, but soon discovered it wouldn't be so easy. Her ears played tricks on her. If the toads were calling for mates, it seemed silly for them to throw their voices. Well, maybe it didn't fool other toads.

She kept turning to fix the position of the clump of bushes that marked the camp. The fire having died out, that was all she had to keep from getting lost. But here the land dipped up and down, and whenever she went down, she lost sight of the bushes. But she always found them when she came up again.

Ah! There it was—a little pool of water at the bottom of a swale, with starlight spattered on its surface.

She had to be careful where she put her feet. As she approached the water, toads hopped in the grass, getting out of her way. She couldn't see them clearly, but she heard them: swish, thump, swish, thump.

And there they were, scores of them, sitting in the puddle, chirping and trilling. Ellayne smiled, and squatted for a better look.

They hopped into and out of the pool, splishing and splashing, blowing themselves up into little balls to force out their music. Ellayne could have grabbed twenty of them as they hopped around her—but she didn't, of course. She'd only come to watch them. The grass was alive with them.

But then she heard something else that drove all thoughts of toads out of her head—

A snort, a clop of hooves and a jingle of harness, and men's soft voices talking.

Ellayne turned, slipping to her hands and knees, and looked up. She saw several riders silhouetted against the night sky, men in flapping cloaks and tall headdresses. The wind carried their speech down to her: she couldn't understand a word of it.

Heathen? A raiding party from across the mountains? She'd heard her father speak of such things. They came looking for slaves and for illegal trade with no tax paid to the state. And they were between her and the camp. If they saw her, she would never see her home again.

Ellayne crept farther down the swale, avoiding the pool, looking for a place to hide. The riders halted to talk among themselves.

There was no place to hide. No, wait—beyond the pool, the land sloped farther down. There were low trees casting dense, dark shadows, exactly what she needed. She aimed for the darkest of the shadows, thankful for the noise made by the toads.

It was waiting for her, a pit of darkness framed by two old bits of wall. She'd be safe there, if only she could reach the place before the riders happened to look in her direction.

Ellayne passed between the ruined walls and found herself on a hard-packed path sloping downward into deeper darkness.

"Wa-la-la-hruuu!" she heard a rider cry. And not waiting to see whether that meant they'd spotted her, she turned and fled into the dark.

Down and down she went, expecting at any moment to hear the horses' hooves behind her. Once she ran into a wall and had to turn to the left. That taught her to go slowly. She knew she'd entered ruins.

Overhead, she saw the stars. It was a relief to know she wasn't underground. Again and again walls rose up in front of her, forcing her to change direction. And as she heard nothing of the riders, her panic died away until at last she dared to stop and listen.

Nothing. They must not have seen her after all. From where she was now, she couldn't even hear the toads. Which meant, she supposed, that she'd gone farther into the ruins than she should have.

Now all she wanted was to get back to camp and go to sleep, so she turned and tried to retrace her steps.

It was impossible.

"Idiot! You got lost!" she muttered to herself.

It was too silly for words. There was the open sky, right over her head. And there she was, between two walls that were too smooth to climb. It was that smooth stone that one so often encountered in these ruins. The walls were too high for her to jump up and grasp the top. If only she had a little something to stand on, so she could climb to the top of the wall and see the way out.

Ellayne tried to find the way, but the endless corridors led around and around, this way and that, and nowhere in particular. By the time her legs were too tired to go another step, her situation no longer struck her as silly.

She slumped down against the cold stone wall, seated on the hard stone floor, hungry and thirsty and ready to cry. She felt tears running down her cheeks. There was no way out of this. She would have been better off whistling to the riders and walking right up to them. Unexpectedly came a memory of her mother tucking her into bed when she was sick, and feeding her nice, hot broth a spoonful at a time. The tears flowed faster.

"God," she said, "I don't know how to pray, but Obst says all we have to do is talk to You, and You'll hear us. I hope You're listening! I'm lost in here, and they don't know where I am, and I can't get out!"

Once she started, she just kept going—talking to God as if He were another person sitting there across from her: another person, listening. She poured out her heart to Him.

She must have fallen asleep praying because the next thing she knew, her mouth was dry, she was stiff and sore all over, the sky above was as blue as the stones in her mother's turquoise bracelet, and she could see.

Not that there was all that much to see: just the bare stone, as clean as if it had been swept. Here and there she could make out ghostly traces of writing on the walls, too faded to be read.

She got up slowly, achingly. There was nothing to eat, nothing to drink; and if she stayed where she was, she would die.

It was a ruin, burn it! There must be someplace where the wall had fallen down, where she could climb out. All she had to do was to keep going until she found it. Once she got back out on the plain, even the water that the toads lived in would be as good as a long drink from the freshest, cleanest, coldest spring.

Ellayne forced herself down the empty corridor. She must have covered miles last night, she thought. Her legs ached, and she didn't dare think about how hungry and thirsty she was. Just keep going, she thought. There had to be a way out.

She wondered what kind of place this was in ancient times. Why was there no roof? If it had had a roof once, and the roof had fallen in, the floor ought to be covered with rubble.

And suddenly she emerged into a wide open space.

Most of it was still in shadow. Surrounded by walls, the space had more entrances from more different directions than Ellayne could count. And it was huge. A strong man might throw a stone from one side to the other, but she couldn't. Everyone in Ninneburky might assemble there, with space left over.

What was this place? Ellayne forgot to be tired or thirsty, pondering its mystery.

Slowly, gingerly, she walked out toward the middle of the empty space. It felt like she was the last person left in all the world. She tried not to make noise, but even her light little steps echoed hollowly.

As her eyes adjusted to the shadows, she could see that there was some kind of decoration on the smooth stone pavement—something painted, perhaps. She'd have to wait until the sun was higher in the sky before she could see it clearly.

She could already see that of the many dozens of blank hallways that led to this open space, no two of them were different: no telling one from another. When she turned, she couldn't decide which was the corridor she'd entered from. They were all exactly alike, and there would be no finding one's way out of them.

A bird shrilled at her from somewhere, making her jump. She spun around to see it, and it kept on calling. But this was no bird—only a dark thing like a large rat racing across the floor. Starving rats might eat a human being: she was sure she'd read that in *Abombalbap*. If every one of those dark doorways should suddenly teem with rats—but what kind of rat ran on its hind legs? And right at her—

"Wytt!"

Ellayne collapsed when she recognized the Omah. Her legs buckled under her. Shrilling and whistling frantically, he pinched her cheeks and pulled her hair with his hard little hands—pulled it hard enough to make her stop blubbering.

"But how did you find me?" she cried. "And where are Jack and Obst? And where am I?" Then she remembered that he couldn't answer her.

He stepped back and chattered angrily at her, almost as good as a real scolding. And then before she could stop him, he turned and ran away. He ran to the nearest place where one wall met another and somehow scrambled straight up to the top. There he paused and whistled and whistled until Ellayne got up and came to him. He looked down and chattered at her.

"You want me to wait right here?" she said. She was sure that was what he meant, but his only answer was to run off again. And because he ran along the topsides of the roofless chamber, she couldn't see him.

"Ellayne!"

That was Jack's voice. It woke her from a light doze: woke her wide awake, instantly. She scrambled to her feet.

"Jack! Where are you?"

"I'm coming," he answered.

He was following Wytt, who got there first, jumped down to the floor, and up into Ellayne's arms. It was a very good thing to hold him again—and even better to see Jack walking along the top of a wall.

"Be careful!"

"It's all right," he said. "Obst is coming. We'll pull you out of there."

She couldn't imagine Obst tiptoeing along the top of the wall like a cat on a fence. But if Jack said he was coming, he was coming—provided he didn't fall off and break a leg.

Jack was right above her now. He dropped to his hands and knees.

"I brought some water," he said. "Don't drop it." He leaned over and dropped the water bag into her hands as Wytt retreated to her shoulder. By the time she was done drinking, Obst was there, too, standing beside Jack.

"Ellayne," he said, "I'm going to stretch my staff down to you. All you have to do is hold onto it, and we'll pull you up. But you mustn't let go."

"I won't!" she said.

She had to pass the waterskin up to Jack first, and then Obst lowered his staff so she could reach it. "Use your feet to brace yourself against the wall," he said. "Ready?"

And before you knew it, he'd pulled her up, and she was standing on top of the wall. It was wider than you would have thought, and no one was in any danger of falling off. Ellayne heaved a great sigh and trembled all over.

"What is this place?" said Jack.

Ellayne was so curious to see it from above that she got up, quaking legs and all.

The view struck her speechless. The whole maze of corridors extended—oh, who could say how far? There were other open spaces in it, but none as big as the open space over which the travelers stood.

In the midst of the vast floor there was an enormous picture that Ellayne hadn't been able to see when she was standing on it.

"What is it?" she said.

"A map of the world," said Obst.

She looked up at him. If he truly understood what the picture on the floor was meant to be, that understanding brought a haunted look to his face.

"What's a map?" Jack said.

"A picture. A chart that shows you how to find your way."

"And that's the world?" Ellayne said.

"The whole world," said the hermit. "Those great fields of blue are the seas of all the world, those splotches of yellow the islands. And the great land masses in brown and green and gold—some are lands that no one's seen for a thousand years."

Pointing with his staff, he showed them the part of the map that represented Obann: all the wide lands between the Imperial River and the River Winter, between the mountains and the Great Sea, with the long marches of the Southern Wilds stretching down to swathes of gold that represented deserts.

It was only a small portion of the whole.

"That's all of it?" Jack cried. "All of Obann?"

"But there's so much more that isn't Obann!" Ellayne said.

"When this map was made," the hermit said, "men of Obann visited all those countries, even the ones across the seas. Then the Empire extended south to the desert and eastward over the mountains to the Great Lakes—you can see them there, those little strips of blue. That's all Heathen country now.

"But come—let's leave this place! I've never heard of it, but it ought to have been famous. Everyone should have heard of it."

They could walk single file along the tops of the walls. Wytt scampered away from them; he knew the way.

"I don't understand," Ellayne said. "This is such a big place—there must be hundreds of people who've seen it. There were riders out on the plain last night. I thought they were Heathen, so I ran in here to get away from them, and I got lost. But if there were riders by night, there must be other riders by day. No one could miss this place in the daytime!"

"You can be sure that many have passed this place without seeing it," Obst said. "And you can be sure that this ruin, whatever it may have been once, has been here for well over a thousand years. I can only think it must have been hidden until just recently, and lately revealed by the power of God. Maybe floods, great winds, or an earthquake laid it bare. I doubt it'll be long before the Temple sends scholars to explore it."

The great open space was not near the center of the maze, but closer to its southern border. Now that the morning was well advanced and the sun well up in the sky, Ellayne could see that the open space wasn't really very far from the place where she'd first entered the maze.

"I must have gone round and round for hours, just following the twists and turns," she said. "I was afraid I'd never find the way out. How did you find me?"

"Wytt tracked you down, then came back and showed us the way," Jack said. "He must have sniffed your trail like a dog."

A few more minutes and they were back on the plain, just short of the forested hills. Ham, tied to a bush, brayed a greeting to them.

"Why do you look so glum, Obst? Everything's all right now," Jack said.

The old man shook his head.

"I'm troubled because I don't understand what we have seen," he said. "I suppose I'm frightened by the vastness of the world. Why has God let us see it again, after hiding it from us for so many centuries?

"The men who made that map were wicked, ungodly, and powerful; and that maze was a seat of their power. It's as if they've reached out across a gulf of time to touch our world today. I would much rather they didn't touch us."

"We'd do better to be afraid of those riders Ellayne saw," Jack said. He untied Ham. "Let's get to the woods and find some food, or we won't be having any supper tonight."

CHAPTER 27

Martis Meets Friends

Having no track to follow, Martis wanted only to get across the plain as fast as he could. After all, he knew where the children were going; and now it seemed the hermit was going with them. It ought to be easy to find people who would remember seeing them.

He parted from Helki with a full pack of food and a full water bag, and marched all night. By dawn he could do no more; he had to stop and sleep. He made camp by rolling himself up in his blanket and sleeping in a rut. He dreamed of giant birds.

It wasn't the outlaws that had scared him, although he knew they would have killed him. Many had tried to kill Martis. Few men in his profession lived to a ripe old age and died in bed. Someday a man he was trying to kill would kill him. He had long accepted that.

But to be snapped up like an insect! The thought of it made his flesh crawl; the dreams made him toss and turn. He had never in his life been so afraid of anything.

The fear of God is the seed of wisdom ...

The verse from the Wisdom Songs flitted through his mind, and he angrily dismissed it. Scripture wouldn't help him now. The fear of enormous killer birds is the beginning of wisdom, he thought, and better a troop of bodyguards than all the prayers in the world.

He crammed down a cheerless bit of food and drink, packed his blanket, and set out again. He hadn't slept well enough, but it couldn't be helped. He would have to keep walking until he gained the hills, then make straight for Bell Mountain. He might be able to get there ahead of the old man and the children. How fast could they go?

As dusk came on, he was still hiking when he heard the approach of horsemen.

He saw them, four of them, coming down the sloping ground straight for him. They must have seen him first. He knew they were Heathen by their headdresses. To try to escape them on foot would be futile, so he stood and waited for them.

Martis greeted the riders after the manner of their tribe, raising both palms and speaking the ritual words of welcome, "*Elamoon elakoom hessalaym, kawaan.*" Which was to say, "Greetings and blessings to you, my brothers." Up close, he recognized the headbands of the Waal Kota, a fierce tribe very active in the slave trade.

"*Hessalym elkoom,*" answered one of the riders. "Who are you who greets us after the manner of a man?"

"One who has been a guest in the tents of the Waal Kota and sworn friendship with the chieftain Mway, son of Kalal." Martis knew their language well and spoke it with a flair. "And he bade me say this, so that any of his braves will know I speak truth: the star of the War God adorns the chieftain's hand." For the Heathen set great store by the stars and planets, deeming them gods, and Mway wore a ruby ring that was a symbol of his hereditary chieftainship.

The leader of the riders dismounted and clasped Martis' hand. "Well met, friend of the Waal Kota!" he said. He must have recognized Martis' Temple insignia, but he ignored it. "I am Dulayl Sawak, son of Ayrah. How may I tell Chief Mway that I helped his friend?"

"At the moment, warrior, I am in sore need of a horse," Martis said.

"Then you shall have mine."

Martis bowed. It would have been a grave insult to have offered payment for the horse. It was a wiry little beast, bred for endurance in hot, dry country, dull brown with white tail and mane and a white star on its forehead. Indeed, it would have been insulting not to accept the gift—although now Dulayl Sawak would be put to the inconvenience of riding double with one of his men until they could steal another horse.

"Have you seen any other travelers on the way, Dulayl? I seek an old man accompanied by two children."

"We have not. In truth, we go in haste and may have overlooked them."

"If I may speed you on any errand you have in hand, warrior, you have but to speak."

"We have nothing to ask of you," Dulayl said. "We have only come to kill a certain man who broke his pledge, and then return."

Martis found himself moved as Dulayl pressed the horse's reins into his hand. Idolaters and moon-worshippers they were, and slavers and murderers to boot, but the well-mannered Heathen was a master of the noble gesture. And he knew how to honor friendships.

"Take care as you travel in this country, brothers,"

Martis said. "There are strange beasts in the land. A gigantic bird killed and ate my horse."

The riders muttered among themselves. Dulayl nodded.

"It is the same on our side of the mountains," he said. "Last month a man came to my master's tent, the only survivor of a caravan from the south. He swore there was a worm in the desert so venomous that even to look on it was death. All the camels died, and then the men. And I myself have seen a great beast, covered with long red hair, pull down a tree to eat the leaves. My men's arrows bounced off it. I am not ashamed to say that I withdrew in haste. We shall indeed be careful, my friend."

With much ceremony, after the manner of the Heathen, they parted, Martis heading northeast on his new horse, Dulayl and his men riding west. Martis was glad Reesh had several times made him his emissary to the tribes beyond the mountains. It was Lord Reesh's policy for the Temple to have many dealings with the Heathen, in secret. The people of Obann would have thought it a great scandal, but it helped to keep the Temple prosperous and well-informed; and the people knew nothing of it.

As soon as he was in the saddle, Martis felt less fearful. Men weren't meant to toil along on foot like ants, he thought. Now he was in command again, his old self. He kicked the horse into an easy trot and grinned up at the evening stars.

―――

Helki had never before killed one of Squint-eye's men. He'd beaten many of them, insulted more, and refused to pay dues; and Latt had sworn to kill him. Now he supposed Latt would have to try to fulfill that vow.

By first light the next morning, Helki decided to follow Martis over the plain. He rarely left Lintum Forest, so he knew the outlaws would spend days combing the woods for him. Let them think he'd gone away for good. He would return when they least expected him and kill a few more of them. Honest people would rejoice.

He cut down some long bunches of heather and set out with them clutched in his hand. Before nightfall he had occasion to use them.

Seeing three Heathen riders in the distance, Helki lay flat on his belly and held up the heather as a screen. They rode past, hardly fifty paces away, and never saw him. One of the horses had two riders, and Helki wondered about that. Had Martis' giant bird come out onto the plain?

He let them pass out of sight, then got up and resumed his trek. Maybe it would be a good thing if he were present when Martis finally caught up to Obst and the children.

As for Obst and the children, they put all their effort into reaching the wooded hills and making a camp under the trees before night fell. Tomorrow they would rest, Obst said, and gather food.

"How far are we from Bell Mountain?" Jack asked, after they'd made a shelter and gotten a fire going.

"As the crow flies, not far at all," Obst said. "But it'll be all uphill from now on, and the closer we get to our goal, the harder the traveling. We won't be able to see our way until we're well up on the shoulders of the mountains."

"Do you think we'll find King Ozias' bell?" Ellayne said.

"I do."

"I wonder what things will be like by the time we come back down again," Jack said. He was thinking, for no reason at all, of an impossible thing—that after the bell was rung, and God heard it, his own mother and father would be waiting for him when he came down from the mountain. Not ghosts, but alive again. But he kept that thought to himself.

"It's better not to ask the Lord what He will do," Obst said. "*'Shall I hide from my beloved what I will do, lest it sear his heart and melt his eyes?'* His is the power to unmake what He has made."

Jack didn't know how to argue with that. Would God send us up the mountain just so that nothing but terrible things would happen? That was what he should have said, but something kept him from saying it.

"Abombalbap met a knight who found a spear chained to a rock with a golden chain," Ellayne said, "and on the rock it said in golden letters that whoever took that spear would ruin a kingdom with it. And that fool of a knight cut the chain and took the spear, and later on he met another knight and jousted with him and killed him with the spear.

"The knight who was killed turned out to be the only son of a good king who was old and sick, and so the king's nephew became king after him—and he was an evil king. The whole kingdom went bad with him. And Abombalbap had to take the spear away from the evil king and throw it into the lake where the Elf Queen lived, to break the curse."

She stopped to catch her breath. Obst shook his head at her.

"If the children of Obann knew the Scriptures half as well as they know nonsense like *Abombalbap*, we might not be on this mission," he said. "But the whole nation has turned away from the Lord."

"My father read me those stories from my book," Ellayne said, "and my father is a good man. He's the chief councilor in our village."

Whatever Obst was going to say to that, he bit it back. But Jack could guess what it would have been, and he supposed Ellayne could, too.

CHAPTER 28

The Scene of a Massacre

These were much thicker, wilder woods than Lintum Forest. "I think Lintum's older," Jack said to Ellayne, as they followed Obst up a very narrow path. "I'll bet it's a lot easier to get lost up here."

Obst paid no attention to their talk. After two days' travel uphill—their first day in the forest, they gathered food and rested—he seemed to be tiring. Jack hadn't thought anything of it, but Ellayne brought it up in a whisper.

"He's old to be doing this," she said. "Maybe too old."

"Too old?"

"People get tired when they're old. My Uncle Flaran used to be the fastest runner in the district—everybody says so. But now he can hardly run a step, and he says it hurts his heart to try. I wonder how old Obst is!"

"He'll be all right," Jack said. But of course he didn't have a big family like Ellayne's, and he didn't know any old people who could tell him what they were like when they were young. The only old person he knew was his teacher, Ashrof; and he thought of Ashrof as someone who'd always been old.

He didn't want to think about Obst being unable to go on, so he changed the subject. "The trees down in Lintum grow a lot taller," he said, "and a lot farther apart. We heard a lot more birds there, too."

"I'd rather be there than here," Ellayne said. "There's so much moss on the trees, and all that green goo on the rotten logs. And I don't like the look of some of those big mushrooms. There's something about these woods that wants to cover you up and never let you out."

"Haven't seen many animals, have we?" Jack said.

For food they had some white mushrooms that Obst said were practically as good as meat, some plump yellow tubers he'd dug up, and a leafy plant he'd plucked out of a pool. His snares had caught nothing. Jack got off one shot with his slingshot at a rabbit, but missed.

"We won't starve," Obst said. "We'll find streams and ponds with fish in them, birds' nests with eggs, and sooner or later we'll catch some meat. And there may be trappers or hunters who'll trade with us."

Just in case they did meet anyone, Obst took some time to cut Ellayne's hair shorter—an operation Wytt observed with great interest. This time the hair was too short for him to fashion into ornaments, but he collected handfuls of it and sat quietly for a long time, studying it.

"I wonder what people will think if he comes back with us to Ninneburky," Ellayne said.

Jack caught the look on Obst's face and read his thought: he was thinking there might not be a town or people to come back to.

On they climbed, always upward. Sometimes Obst had to use his staff to force a way through thickets. Getting the donkey through wasn't easy, and the donkey didn't enjoy it. Pushing against Ham's hindquarters, Jack found it hard to imagine how King Ozias ever got a big bell up to the top of a mountain.

Late in the morning of their third day in the woods, just after they'd battled through a barricade of high ferns, Obst stopped and held up his hand.

"I smell smoke," he said.

"Not a forest fire!" Ellayne cried.

"Shh! It's too damp for a forest fire. Be quiet, and listen."

Ham smelled the smoke, too; he twitched his ears and wrinkled his snout. Wytt climbed up and stood atop the baggage, sniffing the air.

"Too much smoke for a campfire, and not enough for a wildfire," Obst said. "Stay well behind me, you two. Be ready to turn and run."

Jack had his slingshot tucked into his belt and some round stones in his pocket. He gave Ham's lead to Ellayne and made ready to shoot. Obst led the way slowly, trying to make no noise as he thrust aside the foliage. But anyone could hear them coming, Jack thought.

A little farther and you could see the smoke hanging in the air and hear men talking and moving around.

"Hello!" Obst called. "I come in peace." He raised his hands and stepped into a clearing. Jack couldn't see past him. But he could hear someone say, "Steady—it's just an old man."

"The Lord defend you!" Obst said. "What's happened here?"

Jack pressed forward and stood next to Obst, and there stopped short.

This was a camp, but it was all burned out, and there were dead men on the ground, five of them, with blankets over their faces and their feet sticking out. Two men were alive, staring at Obst. They had knives in their hands and pale, frightened faces.

"I have two children with me and a donkey. But please! Who are you, and what happened to these men? Come up, Layne, and let these fellows see all three of us."

Ellayne came up with Ham and stood beside Jack; he heard her gasp. The two men looked them over.

"I reckon they're all right, Tom," said the elder of the two, a grey-haired man with whiskers. To Jack they looked like ordinary woodsmen, the kind of men who often came to Ninneburky with pelts, venison, and wild nuts to sell.

"Did you see anyone else on your way here?" Tom said, his voice high and strained.

"No one," Obst said.

"You were lucky!"

"Come sit with us," the older man said. "My name's Dunnic, and this is my nephew, Tom. We're trappers, and this is our camp. Or was. These—" he motioned to the dead, "were our friends. Maybe you wouldn't mind helping us bury them. Then I reckon we might as well head home."

Jack and Ellayne picked their way around the bodies, careful not to look at them. There were logs and stones to sit on.

"What happened?" Obst asked again when he was seated. Wytt, meanwhile, had disappeared into the underbrush.

"Heathen scouting party," Dunnic said. "They killed everybody, burned the shelters, and made off with everything. They weren't raiders, or they would've searched for our fur and food caches. Didn't find those. I think they mostly wanted to move on in a hurry, with no one here left alive. They were in such a hurry that they missed Tom and me.

"I guess they're looking for unguarded ways over the mountains. Mark my words—come summer, they'll be swarming all over this country like flies on a dead horse. This time it's going to be a full-scale war."

"We hid in a cave," Tom said. "They went right past us, back and forth. Wanted to cut our throats."

The uncle squeezed his nephew's shoulder. "It's all right, Tom—they're gone. Why don't you go down to the hole and fetch the jug of mead? A drink'd do us good."

Tom nodded, and went off a little ways. Dunnic took another long, careful look at his visitors, then turned to Obst.

"I believe in minding my own business," he said. "That's why I've always liked it up in these hills. People don't meddle with each other.

"Still, it's burned unusual to meet an old man with two kids wandering around up here. If you've got any sense, you'll turn around and hurry back down to the lowlands. As of now, this is a dangerous part of the country."

"We're trying to find our way to Bell Mountain," Obst said.

Dunnic grinned. "Bell Mountain, eh? Well, that won't be too hard to find. You're on it."

CHAPTER 29

A Hunter Is Hunted

While he was on foot, Martis had wanted only to cross the plain by the shortest route. Now that he'd been back on horseback for an hour, he decided to change his plans.

The shortest way to Bell Mountain wasn't the best way to go. Radiating out from Silvertown were roads and trails the miners used, some of them cut right into the sides of the mountains. There was, of course, no trail to the top of Bell Mountain, but there was one that would get you onto the mountain's shoulders. Even if he went as far afield as Silvertown, Martis on horseback could easily get up the mountain before an old man and two children on foot. And in Silvertown he'd hear news, if there was any news to be heard. It was the only real town in Obann so far east. It had a chamber house and a prester, with servants, who would do much to oblige the servant of Lord Reesh, the First Prester.

Martis turned due east. Night was falling, but he felt no need of sleep. It was a lovely, clear night with enough of a young moon and starlight to allow him to travel for a few hours longer.

It was good to be in this part of the country again, he thought. He'd last crossed it four years ago on his way to visit the Waal Kota. The mountain air wafting down to the plain was like a bracing drink. The oligarch in charge of these lands never stirred from his townhouse in Obann City, and that bred an independent spirit in the people of the hills. It would be pleasant to enjoy a taste of that again before going up the mountain.

Not for a moment did Martis believe that anyone would find an ancient bell atop the summit of Mount Yul, waiting all these centuries for someone to climb up and ring it. Serious scholars doubted whether such a person as King Ozias had ever really existed. But certainly his bell did not exist! Lord Reesh would have to find some other explanation for his dreams.

Suddenly the horse reared up with a shriek, almost pitching Martis from the saddle.

"Down, you filthy Heathen!" he snarled, tugging the reins to control the startled beast. Then he saw what had startled it.

Striding toward him was the bird.

Its beak gaped hungrily; its long, stout legs ate up the ground between them. Frozen for a moment, Martis managed to turn the horse and kick it into a gallop. It needed little encouraging.

But the bird could gallop, too. Bent low over his horse's neck, Martis cast a look back, over his shoulder. The great killer was gaining on them, coming on impossibly fast for something so massive. He kicked the horse's ribs and screamed.

"Go, go, go!"

Bred for speed, Dulayl's horse laid back its ears and tore across the ground. The wind whistled in Martis' ears and yanked at his hair and whipped it into his eyes; and slowly they left the bird behind. He kept up the gallop long after they were out of sight of it, and only reined in finally because the horse was near to foundering. He pulled up because he had to, or else kill the horse.

"Whoa, Dulayl!"

His own lungs were nearly as empty as the horse's. Gasping, with his heart hammering against his breastbone, he painfully sat up straight and peered out across the landscape.

Nothing. They were all alone.

He slid from the saddle and sank to his hands and knees, and was sick. He almost passed out, but the taste of bile in his mouth revived him.

What a fool he was, thinking it was the same bird he'd encountered in the woods. There must be a population of them in this country. And yet the woodsman who'd saved him from the outlaws had never seen one.

Martis' horse hung its head and panted. Lather covered its hide. He'd have to be rubbed down, and the only cloth Martis had was his blanket. He'd have to cut off a piece and use that. But the horse had saved his life; "it" was now "he," and from now on his name would be Dulayl.

Weakly, Martis staggered to his feet and brought the blanket out of his pack.

"Well done, Dulayl—well done! Your speed saved us," he gasped, speaking the language of the Heathen in the dialect of the Waal Kota. The horse briefly nuzzled him. Before rubbing him down, Martis gave him a drink of water.

His hands trembled; his knees were like molten wax. Was the whole country full of killer birds, or was he just fantastically unlucky to have run into two of them? How many more would he meet before one of them killed him? He couldn't bear the thought of that crushing beak closing on his skull—and couldn't banish it from his mind, either.

"What shall we do, Dulayl?" he said as he rubbed. "If we stay out in the open, you may be able to outrun the birds. If we venture into the woods on the hills, I fear ambush."

He sighed and fell silent, wiping the lather off the horse's hide. He could feel Dulayl's heart beating under his hands. But at last it slowed to normal, and the horse dipped his head to crop a mouthful of grass.

He was almost done with the rubdown when, at an unguessable distance, he heard a harsh cry.

He froze, and his pulse began to pound again. He stood, stiff and still, listening. Dulayl raised his head and pricked up his ears.

Another cry, from a slightly different direction, answered the first. But they'd both come out of the east. Dulayl shifted his feet nervously.

Martis could not have said how he knew it, but those cries were the voices of the giant birds hunting on the plain.

Did they never sleep? Or did the ones living in the forest hunt by day, and the ones on the plain by night?

They're hunting me, Martis thought. What if they can sniff out my trail and find me when I finally have to sleep?

He wrung out the piece of blanket and put it away. "Come, Dulayl," he said. "It's the hills for us, after all."

He led the horse until he couldn't walk, then rode until he couldn't stay awake in the saddle. It was all he could do to remember to hobble Dulayl. He fell asleep on the ground without a fire, still some unknown distance from the hills.

And the birds hunted him all through his dreams.

Helki, too, spent the night on the plain; and Helki, too, saw a giant bird.

It stalked right past him, and looked right at him, and opened its massive beak halfway, as if to warn him not to move. Helki stood his ground, returning the bird's look. He thought that if he had to, he could break the bird's leg with his staff. But he very much hoped he wouldn't have to.

The bird made no move in his direction. Whatever it was hunting, it wasn't him. He watched until it strode out of sight.

Only then did he become aware that he was trembling from head to toe. He threw his staff in the air and caught it, and yowled at the top of his lungs.

"Whee-aaaah!" The whole night rang with it. "Lord God, you have outdone yourself!"

It wasn't much of a prayer, but that was how Obst had taught him how to pray and that was how he did it. He didn't know that proper prayers were only to be made in Assembly under the direction of a prester.

To Helki it was a simple matter: wherever these strange new animals were coming from, it was God who had created them. He knew no better than that, and it was enough for him. God had created him, too—so Obst had taught him—along with everything else in the world. He was overjoyed to see a new creation, and an awesome one at that. A bird that big truly took your breath away.

Far too excited even to try to sleep, Helki made a simple camp for the night, ate and drank beside his fire, and talked to God until he was calm enough to stretch out on the grass and close his eyes.

Martis woke up miserable, having been pursued all through the night by dreadful dreams. The only boon he enjoyed was that he couldn't remember them.

All he could hope to do was to get up the mountain and try to carry out his mission. It was a fool's mission, but he didn't dare abandon it. Lord Reesh expected him to complete it, and without Reesh he was only a masterless assassin.

At least Dulayl seemed rested, ready and willing to go on. Martis forced down a cheerless morsel of bread and climbed back into the saddle.

Ahead lay the hills, green with trees in bud, and above them the mountains, and above them all Bell Mountain with its veil of clouds. Martis was moved to shake a fist at it, then laughed, having embarrassed himself. He patted the horse's neck.

"Dulayl, I once knew a man, brave as a lion in all respects, but with a deadly fear of spiders," he said. "I seem to be turning into such a man."

Dulayl only snorted, and Martis kicked him toward the hills.

CHAPTER 30

The Lost Shall Be Found

Obst helped to bury the slain trappers, a task that took the rest of the day. Jack and Ellayne had nothing to do; the three men didn't want the help of children, and Ellayne didn't want to go near the bodies. When the dead men were in the ground, Obst said a prayer over them.

"What are you doing?" Dunnic said.

"Magic?" asked his nephew.

"You heard me ask the Most High Lord to receive these men's souls," Obst answered. "It's good to pray at a time like this."

"If that was some kind of Heathen prayer, you've brought bad luck on us!" Tom said.

"Quiet, Tom. Old man, are you a prester, or maybe a reciter?"

After fidgeting and doing nothing all afternoon but watch poor Obst help these men dig holes, Jack couldn't stand such foolish talk. He hopped off the stump he'd been sitting on.

"What's the matter with you two?" he cried. "Haven't you ever heard anybody pray before? This is a holy man, a hermit. He prays all the time! His prayers are twice as good as anybody else's."

The trappers stared at him, and Ellayne stared, too, and right away he felt his cheeks reddening. He turned away so they wouldn't see.

"I left the Temple many years ago," Obst said.

"There's some in these hills who'll put a curse on anybody for a penny," Dunnic said, "and a few who say they can do much more than that. And the nearest chamber house is in Silvertown, so Tom and I don't get much of a chance to go to Assembly and hear real prayers. You'll pardon us for not understanding you were doing a kindness.

"We'll spend the night here, and go back down the hill tomorrow. You're welcome to come with us. We have much more food than we can use."

"You'd spend the night here, after what happened?" Ellayne said.

"Why not? The Heathen won't come back. They think they killed us all."

They had a very small fire that night and they all wanted to eat. But the trappers couldn't tell them the way to the top of the mountain.

"Nobody goes to the top," Dunnic said. "Why should they? Why should anybody want to go to the top of a mountain?"

"You'd only fall off," Tom said.

"Nevertheless, we have a reason to go," Obst said.

"And we don't ask to know it!" Dunnic said. "Don't meddle, that's my rule. If you want to go, that's your business, not mine. All I can tell you is to keep on climbing. Once you're up above the tree line, then maybe you'll see the way. There's hunters who go up that far for mountain goat. Maybe you'll meet one of them and he can help you.

But with Heathen scouts in the country, I don't suppose you'll run into any hunters."

Tom gave them a long look. "The Heathen took our mule," he said. "I wonder if you'd be willing to sell us that donkey of yours. You won't be able to take him to the top."

"He's ours!" Ellayne said.

"We need him to carry our things," Obst said.

"It don't matter," Dunnic said. "We'll cache our furs and come back for them when it's safe. We have more than one donkey can carry, anyhow."

The trappers intended an early start, so they laid out their bedrolls and were soon asleep. Obst drifted off into one of his spells. The fire went out, but Jack didn't care to restart it.

"Better not, if there are Heathen around," he said. He'd never seen a Heathen, and wondered what they looked like. "I'll be glad to get away from this place tomorrow."

"You and me both!" Ellayne said. "I wish Wytt would come back. You don't think he's left us, do you?"

"He'll show up as soon as those men have left us."

"If King Ozias could take a bell up the mountain, we ought to be able to take a donkey. I read somewhere that donkeys are good on mountains."

"You worry too much," Jack said. "Go to sleep."

Ellayne soon did fall asleep, and after a while, Jack did, too. It should've been too cold for them to sleep, he thought. Either the nights were getting warmer, or else they were getting used to sleeping out of doors. Jack tried to count the number of days since they'd left Ninneburky, and that was what put him to sleep.

By and by, a little noise woke him.

It was Dunnic and Tom, shouldering their packs and making ready to leave. The sky was just beginning to turn grey, and most of the stars had fled. A smoky mist hung over the camp.

"Hadn't we ought to take the donkey?" he heard Tom whisper.

"That'd be stealing, Tom," the uncle said.

"That old man's a witch or something."

"All the more reason not to steal from him," Dunnic whispered.

"Burn it, they won't be needing that donkey where they're going."

Tom started to move toward Ham, who was tethered to a log and asleep on his feet. Jack was just about to sit up and call an alarm when he heard a familiar angry chitter.

Tom cried out, "Aaah!" and fled the campsite babbling; and his uncle followed after him as best he could, cursing him and calling after him to stop, the both of them crashing through the underbrush. Jack sat up.

There stood Wytt on top of a stump, brandishing his sharp stick and showing his teeth.

"What is it?" Obst said.

"Jack? Jack!" from Ellayne.

Jack was laughing too hard to answer them.

Martis pushed his horse to get up into the hills. Dulayl seemed as anxious to get off the plain as he was, and toiled valiantly. It looked like they would be among the trees by sundown.

Fatigue took some of the edge off Martis' fear. He saw no sign of the killer birds all day. Maybe they didn't like the high ground.

He wondered how far ahead of him the children were. Short legs and old man's legs wouldn't make much speed up a mountain. He ought to be able to catch up to them well before they gained the summit.

Martis had never climbed a high mountain. He knew no one who had. There were men who swam across rivers, raced horses, boxed, wrestled, or bowled tenpins for sport; but no one climbed mountains. So he had no idea what to expect by way of obstacles—except, of course, the cold. There was snow up there even in the summertime. He'd have to do something about getting winter clothes, and probably some furs to wrap around him when he slept.

With his mind so occupied, he startled when Dulayl neighed unexpectedly. And then he saw a child coming toward him down the long slope.

He pulled up sharply, rubbed his eyes. It was a girl, and she was all alone. Was it his girl—Ellayne from Ninneburky? But it had to be. Why was she alone? What had happened to the boy and the old man? She walked slowly, stumbling.

He whistled to her, and waved.

"Hello! Little girl!" he called. "Don't be afraid!"

She stopped, and stood staring at him. Martis dismounted, approached her on foot.

Oddly, she wore a dress of plain brown homespun, much stained and dotted with green burrs. Martis had expected her to be wearing boy's clothes. Her face was dirty, her fair hair flying out in all directions.

"It's all right," he soothed her, lest she try to run away, and force him to chase her. "I won't hurt you. But tell me who you are and what you're doing here all alone. Don't be afraid of me."

She looked up and showed him deep green eyes. He was sure Ellayne had blue eyes. She looked into his eyes and spoke in a surprisingly clear and penetrating voice.

"There is a book missing," she said.

Martis' lips parted, but he couldn't think of anything to say. He couldn't seem to think at all.

"The book that was lost shall be found," she said. Her eyes held him prisoner. "They shall hear all the words of the book. They shall hear my words again."

And then her legs buckled and she fell.

She weighed almost nothing. Martis scooped her up, realized he had nowhere to take her, and gently laid her back down. He sprinkled water on her face and rubbed away some of the grime. He kept doing it until she opened her eyes again. They were a much lighter green than they'd looked at first. Her eyes darted this way and that, and her body trembled.

"Shhh! You're safe now; you're all right," Martis said. "Who are you, child? What's your name? Can you speak to me?"

"Thirsty..." The word barely crawled out of her mouth.

Martis gave her a little sip of water, not too much. He had to minister to her for several minutes before she spoke again.

"Who are you?" she asked.

"Just a traveler. My name is Martis. What's yours?"

"Jandra."

He was sure this was not Ellayne. She didn't fit the description.

"What are you doing out here all alone, Jandra?"

Tears filled her eyes. "Men came," she said. "They burned down the houses. My daddy made me run away. So I just kept running."

Martis understood. There were a few small settlements scattered among the hills. Heathen raiders must have burned one out. Or it might be something more than a raid. The Temple had intelligence that war was brewing.

"Listen, Jandra," he said. "It's almost nighttime. I'm going to take you with me a little ways on my horse, and then we'll make a camp with a fire, and we'll have something to eat. It's not safe to stay out here in the open at night. But I'll take good care of you. All right?"

She nodded. He picked her up and swung into the saddle. He wanted to be under the trees by nightfall, and he'd have to hurry.

She fell asleep in his arms.

What am I going to do now? he wondered. But he wondered even more about her first words to him: *there is a book missing.* He was sure he would be better off never having heard those words.

CHAPTER 31

Of Wolves and Men

Ham's load was a little heavier now, with a plentiful supply of the trappers' dried meat and a pair of treated wolf pelts that would be a comfort on cold nights. But the thought of wolves prowling the woods made Ellayne uneasy.

"There might be werewolves, too," she said.

"What are werewolves?" Jack asked.

"A werewolf is someone who can turn into a wolf. Sometimes there are whole tribes of them, and they hunt down regular people and eat them up. Abombalbap once had to kill a wicked queen who—"

"Peace!" snapped Obst, startling Ellayne into silence. The children had never seen him angry like that. His face seemed to have turned to stone. It was more than a moment before he softened.

"Peace, Ellayne," he said, this time gently. "Our way will be hard and dangerous enough without giving in to pagan superstitions.

"There are no werewolves, and that book of Abombalbap stories has misinstructed you. Hundreds of years ago, there were many books like that. Few have lasted as long as your Abombalbap, but they all had this in common: more than half of what went into them was Heathen. I promise you, real wolves are dangerous enough; and men don't need to turn into wolves to be more dangerous than wolves."

Without another word, he turned and picked a path leading away from the trappers' campsite. The children had no choice but to follow, Jack bringing up the rear with Ham. Wytt rushed ahead, in and out of the underbrush.

"Wait, Obst!" Jack said. "How do you know the way to go? The trees are so thick, we can't see the mountain."

"Our bodies will tell us the right way. It'll be harder and harder, always uphill, and we'll feel it in our legs. If it ever seems to be getting easier, we'll know we're going the wrong way."

"Glad I asked," Jack muttered.

Certainly the way Obst picked for them all day was hard enough, Jack thought. It was maddening, not being able to see the tops of the mountains. After a time they couldn't ask Obst anything more because he was all wrapped up in prayer—in the ancient language of the Scriptures, so you couldn't understand him. But he was right about one thing. It wasn't long before your legs told you that you were climbing.

"I don't see how he knows there's no such thing as werewolves," Ellayne said, when they were lucky enough to hit a trail that was easy enough to permit them to talk. "You said Tom thought Obst might be a witch. He isn't, of course—but why would he say that unless there really were witches in this country?"

"I don't know. What's a witch?" Jack said.

"Really! Sometimes you talk like you don't know anything. A witch is someone who can do magic. Nasty magic."

"I never heard much about magic."

"Oh, there isn't much of it in civilized places. But we're not in civilized places now. We'll be all right, though, because Obst is with us. He's a holy man, and magic won't work against him. It says so in my book."

Jack grinned at her. "But he doesn't think much of your book!"

Ellayne put on a haughty look. "Just because he's holy doesn't mean he knows everything," she said.

The path narrowed again, stickers snatched at their clothes, and they couldn't talk anymore. The trees grew so close together, you could barely see the sky.

Jack plodded on, stung by how much he didn't know. He'd never heard of werewolves, never read a book, and had no idea what magic was. It was all right for Obst to know so much: he was an old man and a scholar. But Ellayne was just a girl, and she knew all about things that Jack had hardly heard of. He felt like a fool.

Someday, he thought, when we come down from the mountaintop, I'll get a roomful of books and read them all. He'd start by making Obst teach him the Scriptures.

It never entered his mind that there might be neither books nor teachers in the world after he'd rung the bell on Bell Mountain.

The little girl fell asleep before Martis could feed her.

They'd reached the trees before nightfall, and he cleared a space for camp and built a fire; but she didn't wait to be fed before sinking into a deep sleep. He let her be.

Now there was no way he could bring her with him up

the mountain, and he couldn't sacrifice his mission by going back and finding someone to take care of her. Martis had never married, never had children of his own, and had no experience with children beyond having been a child himself, once upon a time. He never thought of his childhood, and had no clear memory of it.

As he sat by the fire and nibbled his bread, it struck him that he didn't know some of the simplest things that even the most ordinary people knew. What do you do with a child?

It amazed him that he was even thinking along such lines. Of course the only thing to do was to leave her behind and continue on his journey. Whatever became of her afterward was none of his concern. If she went out on the plain and a big bird made a meal of her, what was that to him?

It was a thought that made his heart grow cold.

"There's something wrong with me, Dulayl," he told the horse, hobbled nearby. "I am an assassin. My calling in life is to kill men whom my master wishes dead. I've killed women, too. And I did it willingly because it made me indispensable to my master and the recipient of his trust. I am an extension of his power, which he exercises for the good of the state. Therefore I am good."

And now, he thought, I'm talking to a horse.

Maybe it would be kinder to kill the girl while she slept. One sharp blow from his mace, and her troubles would be over. She would never know the terror of seeing the feathered mass loom over her, the great beak gaping for her—

He ground his teeth and ground his fists against his skull. What was the matter with him?

"There is a book missing."

He lowered his hands. His mind must be going. To hear those words again, that was not good.

"That which was put away shall be brought to light."

He turned. He wasn't imagining it. Jandra lay on her back, speaking in her sleep. Her voice had power now—not at all the voice of an exhausted, thirsty child.

"My people shall hear all my words that are in the book."

"What book?" Martis said. "What words?"

"My words. They shall hear my words, and they shall seek me."

He crawled closer and bent over her. She was fast asleep; you could tell by looking at her.

"Who are you, child?" he said. "What are you talking about?"

But she spoke no more. She hiccupped once and rolled onto her side, snoring softly.

Martis sat back heavily, trying to reason with himself. The child was half-crazed with grief and hardship. In all probability, raiders had slaughtered her family. She was raving in her sleep. Her words meant nothing.

But they do, argued another voice in his mind. *You know they do.*

I have a mission to attend to, he argued back. There is no place in it for this. Tomorrow I ride on.

The birds will have her.

Biting back a cry, he turned away from her, threw himself down beside the fire, and buried his head in his blanket. Sleep took him unaware; and when next he was aware of anything, his eyes opened to the morning.

Martis rolled over, stiff and sore, and sat up.

The girl was gone.

He struggled to his feet, looked all around. He didn't see her.

"Jandra!"

His call echoed in the stillness of the early morning. Dulayl awoke with a snort.

"Jandra, where are you?"

No answer he received but for a soft, mocking echo among the trees.

"Well," he said to the horse, "she's gone. The matter is out of my hands. I did her no harm, and my hands are clean."

But who cared if his hands were clean? An astonishing claim to make, for a man in his profession! He laughed at himself.

All the same, he had a hollow feeling in his bowels, something he hadn't experienced since his first kill. He hurried to eat, saddle his horse, find a trail, and be on his way.

It was easy enough to leave his camp behind. But whatever it was, that now resided in the pit of his stomach, traveled with him.

CHAPTER 32

In King Ozias' Footsteps

Jack would never have thought climbing Bell Mountain might be dull and tedious work. But it was.

It took them three more days to pass through the wooded approaches to the summit. Without the food the trappers gave them, their journey might have ended there. They found water enough, but the dried meat was all they had to eat.

"I'm not too familiar with this kind of country," Obst admitted, "but certainly I expected to see more game than this. The trappers never wanted for deer or squirrels. Well, I suppose if we stopped traveling, we might catch something we could eat. Maybe we should stop, once the end of this forest is in sight."

The growth was so dense that you couldn't see animals even if you heard them. And often enough, you did—a heavy body crashing through a nearby thicket, hidden birds calling from the treetops, and owls hooting by night. Once they heard a cry that was like a great ox groaning, but Obst couldn't say what that was.

At least Wytt ate well. He went out one night and came back with blood on the point of his stick. He caught bugs and munched on bits of fungi he plucked from rotten logs. And Ham found some of the plants to his liking.

Their third night on the trail, as they sat under their shelter with their campfire dying down, Ellayne said something that greatly troubled Jack.

"How much farther do you think he can go?" she asked. Her eyes pointed to Obst, who'd fallen asleep sitting up with his mouth open. "He looks terrible."

"He's tired, that's all," Jack said. "We're tired, too. It must be hard for him to go in front all the time, finding the way."

"Do you think it'll be easy once we're really going up the mountain?"

"How should I know? I've never climbed a mountain! I guess if King Ozias and a few of his men could drag a big old bell up to the top, we can get there, too."

"It's going to get cold, though. There's always snow at the top."

"If you don't want to go, just say so!" Jack snapped. He was loud, but it didn't wake Obst.

"Oh, don't be a droop. Of course I'm going. We've gone too far to go back, anyhow. We might not even be able to go back."

Jack had no answer to that. It made him think of Ashrof saying that anyone who tried to climb the mountain would freeze to death, or starve, or slip on the ice and fall off, or get eaten by a bear. He'd made it sound so hopeless, and now Ellayne was talking about Obst falling down dead on them before they got to the summit.

"When we come to the end of the woods," he said, after thinking it over, "we'll stop for a while. We'll let Obst rest and get his strength back. We'll set traps and get fresh meat. After that, it can't be too much farther. And we have to go on. I'd rather die than turn back."

After a long pause, Ellayne spoke again.

"I'm thinking of that picture of the world, that map in the ruins where I was lost, and how only a little bit of that whole big picture was Obann. All those seas and faraway countries that don't even have names! If we do get to the top and ring the bell, do you think they'll hear it even across the sea?"

Jack laughed. "Ozias put it there so God would hear it!" he said. "Not people across the sea. I hope God's closer than that."

But where exactly God might be, Jack hardly had words to frame the question.

As if to prove Ellayne right, Obst struggled all the next day. Jack, bringing up the rear, could hear him panting as he led the way. The only trails he could find seemed to fight him, forcing him to push hard with his staff and with his body. It was a warm day, too, and in the afternoon there were tiny flies that wanted nothing but to fly into your eyes and up your nose. Soon Jack and Ellayne were flailing at them, wasting energy.

"They're horrible!" Ellayne cried. "Why don't they go away?"

Obst went on for a little ways, then stopped and bent over. He seemed to be washing his hands, and then his face, but Jack couldn't see what he was really doing.

He straightened up and turned to Ellayne.

"Take these leaves," he said, offering her a handful. "Crush them in your hands and rub the juice on your face. It'll keep off the flies."

He plucked some more and passed them to Jack. The children followed his instructions. The juice from the leaves had a nasty, greasy feel and a strong smell that was not unpleasant—just strong.

"It smells almost like the mint that my aunt likes to put in her tea," Ellayne said.

In a minute or two the flies ceased to trouble them. Obst put his hands to the small of his back, stretched, and sighed.

"Are you all right?" Jack said.

"Only feeling my years." Obst smiled at him, but there were shadows under his eyes. "Let's move on."

Before long their trail widened, and Jack thought the light grew stronger. He looked up and saw big patches of blue sky, more sky than he'd seen for days. He even thought he felt a breath of wind.

A little farther and he could see gaps in the trees straight ahead, revealing strips of sky.

"We're coming out of the woods!" he cried.

And soon they were out, entering a region of widely separated trees—most of them pines with beds of soft needles underneath—and huge, lichen-spotted boulders planted in the earth. In the near distance rose the bare, purple crags and palisades of the mountains, and a delicious breeze caressed their faces.

Ellayne waved her arms in the air and dashed ahead of Obst. "At last! Urrah!" she exulted.

Obst said nothing, only sank wearily onto a stone and closed his eyes.

"Finally! Room to move around!" Ellayne began to do a little dance. Just like a girl, Jack thought. His own legs were too tired for a dance.

Refreshed by the sunlight and the breeze, he let go of Ham's lead and wandered, examining this place that was so different from the woods that had hemmed them in for days. One of the boulders caught his eye. It had a funny shape to it, tall and narrow, with straight sides. He walked up to stand in its shade.

Taking a closer look, he found something that surprised him.

"Obst!" he called. "Come and see this!"

The old man groaned and got up. Jack paid no heed to that, although he might have been alarmed if he could have seen how unsteady Obst was on his feet. But at the moment he had eyes only for the stone.

"What is it?"

Jack startled when Obst laid a hand on his shoulder.

"Look at this!" he said.

Obst looked. The rock was dark, discolored by moss. On its dark side, away from the sun, carved deeply into its surface, were designs that Jack thought must be writing. He couldn't read this kind of writing, whatever it was, but he was sure he knew writing when he saw it.

"It is writing, isn't it?" he said. "Can you read it?"

Obst's fingers tightened on Jack's shoulder, digging in.

"Yes. I can."

Ellayne finally noticed what they were doing, left off her dancing, and joined them. "What are you looking at?" she said.

"Shh!" Jack answered.

Obst's hand began to quiver. Jack turned from the rock and tugged at Obst's robe.

"What is it? What does it say?" he cried.

Obst pointed with his staff. "Do you see that group of markings there—the ones enclosed in a kind of square? That is King Ozias' name, written in characters so ancient that we know them only from the oldest fragments of the Scriptures.

"That much I can read for certain. As for the rest, I doubt that any man can read it fully. Just a character or two, that's all I can recognize. And there's the words for 'the king's road.' But it doesn't matter what else this inscription says. We now know for certain that King Ozias came this way. There's no doubt of it! And that means we're on the right path, too, and our quest is not in vain."

With that he dropped to his knees and prayed, rapidly, in the ancient language of the Scriptures, and became oblivious to all else. Jack reached for Ellayne's hand, and they squeezed each other, hard.

"We're practically there," Ellayne said softly.

"In King Ozias' footsteps," Jack said.

CHAPTER 33

The Flail of the Lord

Dulayl, used to wide-open spaces, did not like traveling under the trees. Martis had to fight him all morning. He would shy at things that rustled in the underbrush, too small and furtive to be seen. Doubtless they were nothing more than mice or wood rats; but Martis wished he could see them, whatever they were.

The horse almost threw him, and he almost let himself be thrown, when they came unexpectedly upon two men hiking toward them on the narrow trail. The men pulled up short, and one of them drew a knife.

"Ho, wait!" cried the elder of the two. "Can't you see he's not a Heathen? Your pardon, stranger—we didn't mean to startle your horse. We don't see many horsemen up here."

Martis got Dulayl under control. He sat erect in the saddle so the men could see his Temple colors.

"No offense taken," he said. "Who are you, and why were you in such a hurry?"

"We could ask the same of you!"

"Hush, Tom. Will you put that knife away? This man comes from the Temple," the older man said. "Sir, we're all that's left of a trapping party, a day's climb up the mountain. Heathen killed the rest. They didn't bother to take our pelts, so they must've been scouts, not raiders. I guess the war we've been hearing about is going to start soon. I wouldn't go any farther up, if I were you."

"I'm looking for an old man with two children," Martis said. "It's Temple business."

"As long as it's Temple business, I'll tell you: we left them at our camp. The old man said they were going to the top of the mountain."

"They'll never get there," Tom said. "And why would they want to?"

"That's a matter for the Temple," Martis said. "I'll thank you to put me on their trail."

The men gave him directions to their camp. There weren't many trails that would take him there. As long as he bore north, he wouldn't be likely to miss it.

"Were you able to tell which nation the Heathen scouts belonged to?" Martis asked.

The older trapper shook his head. "Not without their finery—and I can't tell one dialect from another. My guess would be Abnak Shaar. They're closest."

Martis thanked them and went on his way, and they on theirs. As long as Dulayl could negotiate the trails, he now had an excellent opportunity to overtake the children. This was the closest he'd come to them since he'd started.

But he would have to be careful to avoid the Abnaks. They occupied a poor land along the base of the mountains on the east side, having been forced out of better lands by other nations more numerous; and they were hard to deal with, hasty and combative. They might be allied with the Waal Kota to make war on Obann, but they wouldn't feel bound to honor Chief Mway's friendships. As it was, they had a bad reputation for not respecting the amenities of civilized discourse.

The Temple knew the war was brewing. Every few generations, the Heathen found a leader who could unite their nations in a common purpose. This time it was a prince of the Kuraash, a faraway people who dwelt by the Great Lakes on the eastern edge of the known world. The Temple hadn't yet learned his name—all Obann would know it soon enough, Martis thought—but it was said he possessed a mighty fetish that had been lost for some centuries: an ancient sword belonging to the War God, or some such thing. "Religion is an excellent thing for the common people to believe in," Lord Reesh always said, "as long as it's harnessed to the service of the state." There would be no undirected religious enthusiasms in Obann while he was First Prester.

As for Helki, he strode across the plain from sunup to sundown, his long legs eating up the miles. He followed Martis' trail to a place where it met the trail of four horses. Three went west from there, and one north.

So the Heathen had given Martis one of their horses; that explained why Helki had seen two of them riding double. He wondered how Martis had managed that.

He was surprised when he found the track of Martis' horse turning abruptly to the east. That stopped him.

Why had Martis turned? Had he seen something that made him change his plans? Helki was still pondering it when he saw something that forced him to change his.

It was a child, a little girl all alone, walking straight toward him. She must have been hidden in a dip in the land, or he would have seen her sooner. Not many things unnerved Helki; but the way this child seemed to have appeared out of nowhere came close to doing it.

She was a bit younger than those children who were with Obst, much too young to be walking alone.

"Here, now—what's this?" he spoke to her. She looked at him and kept coming. He went to meet her.

Such a little thing, he thought. Something must have happened to her father and mother.

Helki picked her up. "You shouldn't be wandering around like this," he said. "What's your name?"

She didn't answer. She just looked at him. She had green eyes. Helki looked into them, but didn't find much.

"Don't feel like talking, do you? Well, maybe later." She didn't answer, but at least she didn't seem afraid of him. That was something. "Do you want something to eat?"

She shook her head.

Well, he couldn't follow Martis any farther, not now. Helki had no children of his own, but he had friends who had children, and he knew what was right.

"I'd best get you to people who can take care of you," he said. "I know a family who'd be very nice to a little girl like you. I'll take you to them. They're honest folk who live in a part of Lintum Forest where there are no bad men. It's a long way, though, and it'll take us quite a while to get there. But we'll get there all right."

He watched her carefully as he spoke, and was satisfied that she understood him.

All he could think to do was to deliver her to some settlers he knew, good people who, with a few others, had cleared a little space in the forest and started farms. They were good to their own children, and they'd be good to this poor little thing. Helki certainly couldn't keep her—not with Squint-eye sworn to kill him. She'd have to be kept away from that part of the country.

So Helki dropped his plans and turned back because children had to be taken care of. Even the birds and the beasts knew that, and Helki knew his birds and beasts.

"I hope you'll start to talk to me sometime," he said, as he carried her in long strides across the plain. "I've been kind of lonely out here all by myself."

She snuggled up against his shoulder and fell asleep.

He made a camp for them on the plain, wished he could provide more shelter for her. The fire would have to do. He was lucky to find a spotted snake, which he cooked for her, letting her have all of it. He served it to her bit by bit, and she ate it without a word, licking her fingers after each mouthful.

"Now you mustn't be afraid tonight," he told her. "We've got a nice fire, and I'll keep it going all night long. If any animal comes too close, he'll feel my rod. All you have to do is have a nice sleep."

He'd cut some sheaves of grass to make a bed for her, and he put his shirt over her for a blanket. He'd have a cold night of it, but that would at least keep him awake and alert.

She did fall asleep shortly after her meal, and Helki sat close to the fire. He let the noises of the night soak into his mind, and didn't concern himself with the passage of time.

If need be, he could be on his feet and swinging his staff before his heart beat twice.

He heard when the bats came out in search of insects, heard rodents pattering along their little paths among the tall grass, and all the vagaries of the wind. The least little break in these patterns would arouse him.

"Helki."

The girl sat up and spoke his name. He didn't startle, but he turned at once to face her. He was sure he hadn't told her what his name was.

"You shall be the flail of the Lord," she said. "You shall smite the wicked, and they shall flee from you because I have set you over them." Her eyes glowed like jewels in the firelight.

Helki's bare skin tingled, but it wasn't from the cold.

"If you will obey me, and spare the meek, and deliver the humble from oppression, I will preserve you from all evil."

"I will," he said, for he knew it was no little girl who spoke to him so. He did not know how he knew. That didn't matter.

He waited for more, but she only closed her eyes and sank back into sleep. He crawled to her and tucked his shirt up under her chin.

He knew what Obst would say: it was the voice of God speaking to him through this child, telling him things he didn't understand as yet. Obst talked to God every day.

"Of course He answers me," he would say, when Helki asked him. "I can't tell you how. Sometimes it seems I hear Him in the wind, or simply in the air. Sometimes His voice seems to be coming from the earth, or even from somewhere in my own body. And sometimes it's just as if another man were speaking to me—but of course I can't see Him."

"Why not?"

"Because God is not a man, or a tree, or a gust of wind, or anything that I can see. He made all those things, but He is not any of those things. He is spirit. It is not given to man to see His face."

Helki did not understand what a spirit was; but he reckoned he was now on his way to finding out.

CHAPTER 34

Obst Must Stay Behind

They rested by King Ozias' Stone, as they came to call it, and they foraged for food. Their first morning there, in one of the snares, they caught a fat mountain marmot that made for a royal supper that evening. Obst showed the children a plant that had tasty roots, a few mushrooms that were safe to eat, and berry bushes that might be in fruit before too much longer: those that caught the most sun were already showing little white blossoms.

But this activity of his was all in little bursts, soon over. Mostly he knelt in front of the Stone. The next day he said Jack now knew enough about the snares to manage without him, and he spent the whole day staring at the carven letters. The children couldn't get a word out of him. The few times his lips moved, he uttered nothing but lines of ancient Scripture.

"We should get going," Ellayne said, after they'd failed in repeated attempts to get Obst's attention. "We can't just stay here until it's summer. What if some of those Heathen come?"

"You're the one who said he needed rest," Jack said.

"Does he look like he's resting? I think he looks worse than he did two days ago."

She was right, although Jack didn't want to admit it. There were beads of sweat all over his face, even though there was a cool breeze blowing. He'd gone all pale, too. He looked sick, Jack thought. He remembered a time last year when Van took sick and couldn't work and Jack had to take care of him.

As if to confirm Ellayne's fears, Obst groaned and toppled onto his side.

"Oh, no!" Jack cried. "Come on, let's see if we can drag him to the shelter."

"Are you daft? He's a grown man."

"Well, we can't leave him here with the wind blowing on him!"

They each took an arm. He weighed nowhere near as much as they expected, and without too much of a struggle they were able to pull him to his bed of ferns. Ellayne felt his forehead.

"This is bad," she said. "He has a fever. Whenever I have a fever, my mother puts me to bed."

"We don't have a bed. Put the blanket over him."

They wet a rag and wiped his face. Wytt came over and squatted beside him, gravely watching the proceedings.

Jack took care of Van by feeding him soup and keeping him out of drafts. That was all he knew to do, and up here on the mountain, they couldn't do either.

"What are we going to do?" Ellayne said. She'd gone a little pale, too.

"Burned if I know! Pray that he gets better."

There were already tears in her eyes. A lot of good that'll do, Jack thought, ignoring the tears that blurred his own.

They'd left Ninneburky fully resolved to ascend the mountain on their own, just the two of them, without help from anyone. But by now they'd come to rely on Obst, and for all they knew, he was dying.

The old man's eyes came back into focus, and he startled them by speaking.

"Listen, children," he said. And they had to listen hard because his voice was none too strong. "I have read the writing on the Stone, all of it. The spirit of the Lord was with me—that, and the studies of my youth. I've read it all, and now I know what you must do."

"I thought you said you couldn't read it," Jack said.

"But I can read it now. Listen!

"When King Ozias climbed the mountain, he knew that someday, by the will of God, there would be someone to follow him. So he had his servants carve a message on the Stone, and carve its sides smooth so that someone would notice it.

"Children, the king has marked the way to the summit! You'll find more stones with signs carved into them to show you the way to go. These will lead you safely to the top—to the bell. You must follow the signs, and go up."

"We will—as soon as you're better," Jack said.

Obst smiled at him. "It has not been given to me to go up to the top, my friends. My Lord wishes me to remain here. Why, I don't know.

"The writing on the Stone says that King Ozias went up and came back down, marking his route as he returned. That's how we know we can trust his signs. The way is safe and sure. You won't need me to get up there."

"But we do need you!" Ellayne said. "We can't just leave you here. You might die. Someone has to take care of you."

"Ellayne, Ellayne—I'm a very old man. Had I stayed where I was when you met me, I wouldn't have lived much longer. Indeed, I'm amazed I had the strength to come this far.

"Listen to me, children. This is as far as I can go, but I don't think I'll die for some days yet. There's good water nearby and food that I can gather with very little effort. I doubt I'll die before you ring the bell. And if I die hearing it, I'll be a happy man."

"Happy that the world is going to come to an end?" Ellayne cried.

"No. Happy knowing that I've served the Most High Lord and been obedient to the end of my days. He wishes me to remain here, and I'll be obedient in that.

"But you must be obedient, too. You must go to the top and ring the bell. That's what He wants you to do. As for me, I belong to Him, and He can have me."

"But if you die—"

"Jack, everybody dies. There's no avoiding it. But it's monstrous that the Temple no longer teaches what all the Scriptures say: that we who belong to God belong to Him forever."

Jack looked at Ellayne, and she looked back. They'd never heard anything like that before.

"In the end," Obst said, "the only wisdom we have is to obey."

He seemed comfortable enough that night. The snares had all caught game during the day: mountain squirrels, a fine rock hen, and a young marmot. Obst was able to instruct the children in how to clean and prepare it all to serve as food for several days.

"The worst thing you'll have to deal with is the cold," he told them, "especially once you're up among the clouds. So be sure to take the wolf pelts with you! You'll have a marked path to follow, and better than that, the Lord's protection. You shouldn't have to spend but one night on the way up, and one more on your way down. Load Ham up with plenty of firewood. Ellayne has gotten quite good at getting a fire started. You'll be all right."

They had the marmot for their supper, and Obst went right to sleep afterward. He still looked pale, but at least his forehead wasn't hot anymore.

"I don't know how I'll be able to get to sleep tonight," Ellayne said.

"You heard what he said: we're only two days from the top," Jack said. "We can't stop here. Maybe if we hurry, Obst'll still be alive when we get back. Maybe we can save him."

"If there's anything to come back to," Ellayne said. "You know he thinks God's going to end the whole world this time. Remember the Children of Geb. At least God gave them stepping stones. What kind of stepping stones will we have?"

Jack frowned. "We don't know anything," he said. "It'd take us years just to learn how to read the Old Books, and the rest of our lives to understand them. We can't wait that long."

"No, I guess we can't."

Obst sat up to see them off the next morning. Somehow they'd slept. He used a stick to draw on the ground the signs they should look for on the way, carved into stone. They were simple enough to remember.

"Do you feel any better?" Ellayne asked.

"I feel much better, knowing that you're on your way," Obst said. "I'll probably sleep most of the day. I think I may have eaten too much last night."

It was shaping up to be a fine, sunny day. They were already higher than many of Bell Mountain's consorts, and no longer had to wait for the sun to rise above them. Down on the plains, it would still be dark.

"Go now," Obst said. "You know the way to the next marker. Follow the path. Go!"

They went, leaving him sitting in the shelter.

CHAPTER 35

An Assassin's Conscience

While Obst and the children rested by King Ozias' Stone, Martis forced his way up the mountain through the dense woods and marveled that an old man and two children had come so far on foot.

After the plains, he found the shade and the confinement oppressive; but at least this country was no place for gigantic killer birds. Any animal bigger than a wildcat would have a hard time making its way through the dense growth. Then again, he thought, something must have made these paths I'm using.

He found the camp where the Abnaks killed the trappers, and the fresh graves that Obst had helped dig. It was a dreary place, and he would have to stop there for the night, which was almost upon him. There was plenty of firewood lying about, and someone had erected a lean-to after the Abnaks destroyed the trappers' cabin.

When night descended on those hills, a man who had no fire might as well be blind. Martis sat close to his fire, with Dulayl, hobbled and tethered to a log, to keep him company. He spoke to the horse in the Waal Kota dialect, in case there were Heathen scouts in the woods listening.

"Do you know, Dulayl, there are many people in Obann who wouldn't dream of walking through a graveyard at night? Let alone sleeping by one! Unlike the wise Waal Kota, they're afraid of ghosts. And we of the Temple have done nothing to disabuse them of it.

"Why do you suppose that is, my friend? We could surely teach them that there's nothing in the Scripture to warrant a belief in ghosts: indeed, there are many verses that say that under no circumstances are the dead permitted to return. And yet we let them go right on being afraid of ghosts because it has nothing to do with our higher purpose.

"And what is that purpose? I'm afraid I don't know anymore!"

He laughed aloud—and at once fell silent again because the echo of his laugh among the trees was hideous.

I am coming unraveled, he thought. Giant birds and missing books, they've undone me.

He wondered if the little girl was still alive, Jandra, with her missing book. She wasn't even old enough to read a book. Out of her head, she must have been repeating something she'd heard her father say. Maybe her father had some Scripture memorized. But Martis couldn't think of any verses that matched Jandra's words.

Well, if a bird didn't get her, she'd die of exposure or starvation.

As Martis slowly grew drowsy, his thoughts reverted to the nearby graves. They held the bodies of five men who'd been killed, who'd probably gone to their deaths in terror and astonishment. As the superstitious had it, ghosts were people who couldn't believe they were dead.

Martis didn't believe in ghosts, for the excellent reason that he didn't believe in any kind of life after death at all. Better to be the assassin than the victim, he always said. And so the killings he'd done over the years had never troubled him—until now.

"We humor the people with a belief in an afterlife," Lord Reesh often said. "It gives them something to hope for—indeed, for some of them, poor brutes, the only thing they can hope for. Let them think they'll go on to some ethereal existence as a happy spirit. You can wring that much out of the Scriptures, if you try.

"But we must never so humor ourselves, my boy. Remember that it's better to live and die a servant of the Temple than a slave or an impoverished peasant. Live as long and as well as possible. That's all a man can ask."

Such teachings had always struck Martis as eminently wise, and for most of his life he'd lived by them. But tonight some perverse spirit called up in his mind the faces and the voices of his victims, and reminded him that he had many more than five to answer for.

No! Not to answer for, he argued wearily with himself. I am, and they are not. That's all the answer I need.

In this frame of mind he nodded off to sleep before he could even lie down. As in a fever dream, he tried to count the persons he'd killed in the service of Lord Reesh. By poison, by a dagger in the dark, by the garrote and by drowning, by the clever arrangement of an accident on the city streets and by the suborning of false witnesses in a capital trial—he could count the methods, but every time he came close to tallying up the bodies, he would lose count and have to start again.

Dulayl screamed; and there is nothing to wake a man like the scream of a horse in mortal terror.

Half in a daze, Martis dove for the reins and caught them. Dulayl's struggles to escape jarred him to full wakefulness. He hung on to the leather straps for dear life and tried to get to his feet.

A low, thunderous growl responded to the horse's screams.

There was still some life in the campfire, and by its light Martis saw what at first he thought was a bear pawing at the graves. But it was not a bear.

Dark and huge and lumpy as a bear, but with a small head and long, powerful forelegs and a tail that was like a pillar braced against the ground, the beast interrupted its digging to glare at him with small, cold eyes like little red lanterns and to growl at the horse. It had come for the dead, to pry them from their graves. And it shot into Martis' dream-befuddled mind that when the beast opened the graves, then he would have an exact count of his victims. They were all down there in the ground, waiting to be dug up, waiting to confront him.

The beast rose up on its hind legs, propped up by its tail, and then dropped onto all fours again.

Martis didn't try to mount his panicked horse; that would have been suicidal. It was all he could do to drag the hobbled horse into the nearest opening among the trees and lead him away from the accursed site. The beast at the graves grunted like a giant pig, but made no attempt to pursue them.

By blind chance they hit upon a trail. Martis fought the horse every step of the way, pleading with him to settle down. At long last, Dulayl planted all four hooves on the ground and allowed Martis to slip off the hobble.

Martis climbed onto his back. There was no saddle, but he clung to the bare back somehow, and Dulayl set off along the trail, too weary and too hemmed in to gallop, but too frightened to stay in one place. Martis let him have his way. He couldn't see a thing; he doubted the horse could either. He discovered he was sobbing, but he couldn't seem to stop it.

Dulayl went on until he could go no farther. Martis drifted in and out of sleep, but by some miracle never fell off Dulayl's back. They didn't stop until grey morning began to filter down to the forest floor. Dulayl encountered a spring welling up from the earth, and stopped to drink. Martis slid off his back and knelt beside him, drank from cupped hands, and rubbed cold water over his face until he could keep his eyes open.

He paused to take stock of his situation. He'd lost his pack, his food, his water bag, his blanket, and his saddle. He still had his horse, his clothes, and, thanks to Helki, his mace and his knife.

"Well, old friend," he gasped. "Are we farther up the mountain, or have we lost our way and gone back down?"

There was no way to tell. Martis shivered. He would have given much for his blanket, a fire, and something warm to eat.

"I don't blame you for being afraid of the beast—although a bear or a mountain lion might have been worse," he said. In the stillness of that morning, the sound of his own voice comforted him. "What was it that came out of the woods to eat the dead? Have our nightmares taken the form of fabulous beasts and come to life? I am sure I never heard of any animal with a tail like that."

Only because he had to, he let the horse rest until the sun was high in the sky and the chill was baked away. Then he took the reins and led Dulayl, selecting a path that led upward amid thick brambles. How far they would have to trudge before they cleared the tree line was something that could not be known. Sooner or later, he thought, he would be reduced to eating mushrooms. And if he ate one that was poisonous—well, he would be one with his victims.

But the sun had not yet climbed past noon when the path led him to a place where the trees thinned out and there were only pines, and he could see bare mountains near at hand and feel the sun on his face.

And there, large as life, he found a recently constructed shelter with someone sleeping in it.

CHAPTER 36

Up the Mountain

There was a path, and Jack and Ellayne followed it as it led them higher and higher. Sometimes it led them through passages between great boulders like the walls of houses built close together; and there they found King Ozias' sign scratched deeply into the rock. And sometimes it would bring them close to the edge of a cliff. They paused at the first cliff and looked down.

"Kind of dreary, isn't it?" Jack said.

Below them stretched Bell Mountain's wooded skirts, looking like thick scum on the surface of a stagnant pond. Below that lay the plains, all grey and yellow. Beyond the plains, the world gradually vanished in a smoky haze. It made Jack think of a poor man's carpet, all scuffed and dirty and ready to be thrown out.

"Well, we're too high up to see much," Ellayne said. "It's a long way down."

If you looked up, you couldn't see the summit—just a cloak of hanging fog, the cloud that crowned Bell Mountain. Sometime tomorrow they would be entering that cloud. It didn't look very inviting.

"The sooner we get up, the sooner we can go back down," Jack said. "Come on."

They'd been at it since early in the morning, pushing themselves, and now it was the beginning of the afternoon. Between glimpses of the worn-out, weary world below and the looming cloud above, their spirits flagged. Obst was much in their minds, although neither of them chose to speak of him.

Jack tried to imagine King Ozias coming this way a thousand years ago, or whenever it was, dragging a great heavy bell behind him. Whatever had given him such a mad idea? The men who followed him must have been as mad as he was, carrying that burden through the forest.

Once he caught a glimpse of Ellayne's face and saw her lips moving. How do you like that? he thought. She's praying, just like Obst. That's what he'd be doing now, if he were with us.

Praying didn't seem like such an odd thing to be doing, under the circumstances. All you had to do was talk to God, Obst said, and He would hear you—even if you didn't talk out loud. By and by Jack prayed, too: silently.

God, he prayed, I still don't know why You've sent us here to do this. I don't know why You sent me the dreams and picked me and Ellayne to ring Ozias' bell. Why us? We're only kids. Couldn't you find a grown-up man to do it, or a hero?

But I'm glad you picked us, even though I'm burned if I know why I'm glad.

He wondered what he would do if God talked back to him, like Obst said He did sometimes. He wondered why Obst wasn't terrified when that happened. Jack was sure he'd be, if it happened to him. God's voice, coming out of nowhere—

"Jack!"

He startled, but it was only Ellayne.

"Are you all right?" she said. "You didn't answer me."

"I was praying." And how foolish that would have sounded not too long ago. But up here on the mountain it didn't sound foolish at all.

"I was just wondering how we'd ever have found the right way without the signs," Ellayne said. "Look over there—up a ways."

Jack looked where she pointed and saw there was a deep gorge between them and another shoulder of the mountain. That way was as smooth as glass and tilted upward at a very sharp angle. Above it towered steep crags like a stone wall built by giants.

"No getting up that way," he said.

"We'll have to stop soon and make a fire. The sun's on its way down. There's already a chill in the air."

"Let's go just a little farther. Just until we find a better place to sleep."

For a moment Martis thought the old man lying in the shelter was dead. But when he squatted down beside him, the man opened his eyes and said, "Hello!"

"Are you Obst, the hermit?"

"I am. And you wear the insignia of the Temple. That's funny!"

That remark irritated Martis, but he ignored it. "Where are the children?"

"On their way to the top of the mountain. But you must know all about that, or you wouldn't be here."

"Which way did they go?"

"Young man, you look all done in. Jack and Ellayne are quite a few hours ahead of you, and you'll never catch up to them unless you rest first and recover some of your strength. I have food here and a place to sleep. Have something to eat and rest yourself; and then I'll tell you which way to go. There's only one safe way to the top."

"I'd rather you told me that now," Martis said.

"You'd only go stumbling off to your own destruction. Rest first. You look worse than I feel, and I'm dying."

Ordinarily Martis would have used force to make the old man tell him the way, with no more thought than he would have expended to squeeze the last few drops of water out of a damp rag. Pain was always a powerful persuader. But this time he refrained from violence—why, he couldn't have said.

"I want to be there when they ring the bell," he said.

"It'll be a clear night tonight with a nearly full moon," Obst said. "You can make your climb then, and make up the distance while Jack and Ellayne are sleeping. The cold will be cruel, and you'll need all your strength. But I think you'll be there when they ring the bell if God has brought you this far. Meanwhile, you should rest. I can see how badly you need it."

Surprised at himself, Martis acquiesced. There was a small store of fresh-caught game. Martis started a fire, spitted a skinned squirrel, and roasted it over the flame.

Perhaps because the old man was dying and would die up here and never repeat it to another living soul, Martis found himself telling him all that had happened to him since he set out from Ninneburky. Once he'd started, he couldn't hold it back. He could not remember the last time he'd talked so much about himself—or if he ever had. He couldn't stop.

He might have, had the old man commented on anything he said. But Obst held his peace, listening intently. To Lord Reesh, his patron, Martis would never have confessed to a single moment of weakness. Reesh would not have had the patience for it: Martis' feelings could be of no use to him.

Only once did Obst speak, and then only because Martis asked a question.

"I hardly understand myself anymore," he was saying. "The little girl was nothing to me. I couldn't abandon my mission for her sake. But now she haunts me. I keep hearing her say, 'There is a book missing.' Why did she say that? What could it mean?"

He paused there, and at last the hermit spoke.

"But surely you know what she meant," he said. "Were you not schooled in the Temple? Haven't you studied the Scriptures?"

Martis shrugged. When Reesh took him into his service, he was little more than a boy, a cutpurse and a pickpocket on his way to a short career as a thief, and then the gallows or the slave pens. Reesh taught him to read and write, but made no scholar of him.

"I never studied to be a reciter or a prester," he said.

"Then know this," Obst said. "There were bad times during the age of the Empire, and worse times between the fall of the kingdom and the rise of the Empire. Not only did the Temple lie in ruins. There was a great falling away from faith, and persecution of the faithful."

"Yes, but the Temple was rebuilt—"

Obst overrode him. "Not all that was put away has been recovered," he said. "To this day, there are writings that are mentioned in the Scriptures but that no one has read for two thousand years. That's what the girl was telling you. There is a book missing—a Book of Scripture. It's been missing for all this time, but it will soon be found again. That's what she meant."

Martis rebelled. "Absurd! How could a mere child think of a thing like that? A toddler, a baby—"

"Babes and children, old men and old women, and slaves, and the wretched of this world: they shall all speak words of prophecy," Obst said. "They'll all receive visions from the Lord, when the day of the Lord is at hand. Didn't you know that? Why else do you suppose Jack and Ellayne came up this mountain? Not scholars, not presters. A boy and a girl!"

Obst cited fascicles and verses from the Wisdom Songs and half the books of the Prophets. Martis listened, stunned.

Reesh should have told him this. Why hadn't he? Was the First Prester's unbelief so fragile that he had to protect it by pretending not to see or hear?

"I suppose there is much you haven't told me about yourself and your reason for coming here," Obst said. "No matter. God brought you here. You wouldn't be here otherwise. Your terrible bird would have devoured you. And God meant for you and me to meet and have this conversation.

"But I'm tired now, and I want to go back to sleep. I suggest you do the same. Wake me at moonrise, and I'll tell you how to find the children."

The old man rolled onto his side and shut his eyes. In his imagination Martis heard Lord Reesh shouting, "Throttle him, you fool! Prod him with a heated knife, and make him tell you now!"

For the first time in his life, Martis didn't listen to his master. He shut his mind and was soon asleep under the shelter beside the hermit.

CHAPTER 37

Night on the Mountain

Jack and Ellayne found a place to sleep that might have been created for that very purpose. High boulders sheltered it on one side and a towering scarp on the other. Tough grass grew there in thick tussocks. They cut armfuls of it to cushion them against the stony breast of the mountain.

All around this place were King Ozias' signs, carved into the rock.

"What a pity we can't read it!" Ellayne said.

"But I'm sure this must be the spot where Ozias spent his night on the mountain," Jack said.

"It says in my book that King Ozias had more adventures than Abombalbap, and harder ones."

"Does your book say what happened to him after he came down from the mountain?"

Ellayne shook her head. Jack wished he knew the Old Books better. Ozias was the last king, the very last, and the only one of the latter kings who pleased God. That was what Ashrof said. "Blessed forever, say the Scriptures. King Ozias the Blessed."

God had a funny way of showing blessedness, Jack thought. Of course, he didn't know the whole story of Ozias' life, just the bits that Ashrof had taught him. How the usurpers tried to kill the queen before her child could be born, and how she'd had to flee to Lintum Forest where Ozias was born. How his enemies hunted him all the days of his life, and how he finally became king, in spite of all of them. And he gave thanks to God, and ruled with justice and mercy, and beat down the Heathen, and composed so many of the Wisdom Songs. But the rebels made a compact with the Heathen and drove King Ozias from his throne. They sought his life. They hunted him up and down Obann, he and his little band of faithful men. But he escaped them always, time and again—

And that was all there was to it.

"It isn't right that he just disappeared," Jack said. "Where did he go from here? How long did he live, and how did he die? Ashrof wasn't even sure Ozias climbed this mountain. He said the Scriptures don't say, one way or the other."

"Well, we know he did because here are his signs," Ellayne said.

"He went up and came down—and that's all that anybody knows. There ought to be more to it," Jack said. "There ought to be an end to the story. It shouldn't just stop before it comes to the end."

Ellayne looked up at the grey sky, and shivered. "We'd better get the fire started," she said.

They found a sheltered bay among some house-sized boulders, and there they built their fire, spread their grass, and had their supper, the rest of the marmot. Ham munched happily on the mountain grass. Wytt, who'd been riding atop the firewood all day, scurried off to explore.

It was going to be a cold night, but the children had their winter clothes, the wolf pelts, and their fire. And when the last trace of daylight fled, the stars came marching out in endless armies. Jack and Ellayne looked up at more stars than they'd ever seen in their lives; looked and looked, and always more to see—until clouds rode across the sky and hid the stars. In a moment it was as if the stars were only something that they'd dreamed or just imagined.

Jack couldn't bring himself to speak. His mind was carrying one big thought and couldn't carry any more.

Tomorrow they'd be going to the top. Climbing up into the cloud that hid the summit, passing out of sight and knowledge of the world; and there they would find King Ozias' bell—the bell that God Himself would hear when they rang it.

Under the stars, Martis toiled along the trail to the summit, sometimes riding, mostly leading Dulayl where the way was steep. He probably should have left the horse behind, but then he would have been alone.

Being alone had never troubled Martis. He'd been alone all his life. The closest thing he had to a friend was Lord Reesh—a thought that brought a wry smile to Martis' lips. Dulayl was more of a friend than Reesh could ever be, and Dulayl was only a horse. Martis knew that the day he ceased to be useful to Reesh, the First Prester would find a new assassin and tell him to bury the old one. That was how Martis had gained his position in the first place.

Being alone troubled him tonight. He was more alone than the mad old man he'd left dying in a lean-to.

"But I'm not alone," Obst said when they parted. "My Lord is with me constantly. I've never been so close to Him."

Which was all very well for the likes of Obst, who had not been taught by the First Prester himself that God was at most "a part of us that strives to be more than flesh and blood"—but how could it comfort a man like Martis, who believed he knew better? What was prayer but a form of talking to oneself?

Well, at least the signs were where Obst said they'd be, and there was enough light provided by the moon and stars to see them. And the labor of the climb made for an effective protection from the cold. Martis' hands and face got a little numb, but the rest of him was warm enough.

He was sure he was making better time than the children could have, if only by virtue of his longer strides. He had to discipline himself not to try too hard, lest he use up his strength before he reached the summit.

The one thing he couldn't control, and couldn't fight, was a sense of being exposed. Like a spider crawling across a spotless tablecloth, he thought, with no hope of escaping notice the moment someone chanced to look in his direction, and no sooner seen than killed. He felt more exposed here than he'd ever felt on the plain. This sensation preyed on him and turned every trick of the wind, every echo of a footfall, into a nameless menace.

"Losing my nerve, Dulayl—that's what's wrong with me," he said. "Next thing you know, I'll be praying like that poor old man. His nerve's just fine, thank you!"

Sometimes he looked up at the dense cloud that concealed the journey's end. God lived in a cloud like that, he thought, or so the children of Geb believed, thousands of years ago, according to the Book of Beginnings.

That'd be a laugh on me, he said to himself, if God lived in this cloud and I walked right into it!

And God would prove to be the biggest of all the killer birds, with gaping beak and burning eyes, and a man and his horse would go down in a single gulp.

Jack woke to a sense of having passed through some moment of indescribable sweetness, but he couldn't remember what it was. A dream that blew away like smoke the moment he stirred his eyelids—no hope of calling it back. He looked up into a pearly sky that was like a bowl of milk.

Ellayne was already working to restart the fire, still huddled in her wolfskin. When Jack sat up, she turned and grinned at him.

"What a s-s-sleepyhead!" she said, with her teeth chattering a little. "I don't know how I slept at all last night, but I did."

"Look at the sky," Jack said. Now that he was up, he felt the cold. "I wonder if it's going to snow."

"That's not the sky. It's the cloud."

"Oh."

Ellayne got the fire going, fed it, built it up. Jack stared into the cloud. It covered the whole sky.

"I hope we'll still be able to see once we're inside it," he said.

"King Ozias and his men went into the cloud and came out again."

"I'm just thinking it'd be too bad if we couldn't find the bell once we were up there."

"I'd give anything for a cup of hot tea, with honey in it," Ellayne said.

Jack helped her stoke the fire. Once they'd had their breakfast, a mountain squirrel, and then moved around a bit, they stopped shivering.

"I think we'd better leave Ham here," Jack said. "There's grass for him and some shelter if the weather turns bad. We don't need to be carting a load of firewood to the top. This is where we'll stop again when we come back down."

Wytt popped out from a cozy nest he'd made among the baggage. He chattered at them. Ellayne chattered back, and he came to her. She picked him up and held him.

"You don't have to come up to the top, Wytt," she said. "We'll be coming right back down again."

He replied with a long string of barks and whistles.

"He'll do as he pleases. He always does," Jack said. "Maybe he can keep Ham company."

"Do you really think we should leave Ham?" Ellayne cast a worried glance at the donkey, who was feeding again.

"It's only for a little while. He might be afraid inside the cloud."

"We might be afraid, too! But I suppose you're right."

They made their last few preparations, dressing as warmly as they could, taking nothing with them but the big knife and a couple of stout sticks. Jack wished they had some rope, but they didn't. The last thing he did was to hobble the donkey and kiss its muzzle.

"We'll be right back, Ham," he said. "You rest. It's your day off."

Wytt hopped away from Ellayne and burrowed into her wolfskin. Just his face stuck out. He blinked at them and showed his teeth.

"That's that, then," she said.

And Jack said, "Let's go ring the bell."

CHAPTER 38

Into the Cloud

As the new day crept up on the high peaks of the mountains, all the broad lands below them still lay wrapped in night.

The rivers flowed as always, seeking the sea; and the sea's waves lapped the shore; but these things knew no season. All along the Imperial River, the towns and ports lay with their doors shut and their streets deserted. No laborers toiled on the docks; no herdsmen gathered their herds together; no carters drove their carts along the roads. In the great city of Obann, a few watchmen in a few great houses yawned and looked forward to the sunrise when their watch would end. Soon enough the towns, the villages, the farms, and the logging camps, and the great city itself would rouse to the rising of the sun, and the people would go about the business of another day.

For Jack and Ellayne, high up on the mountain, the day had already begun. While the people in the lowlands slept out the remainder of the night, Jack and Ellayne followed King Ozias' trail.

The going was steep, now, very steep indeed, and they soon felt it in their legs. No more grass grew anywhere; the only sign of life was lichen plastered to the rock. All under their feet was bare rock, here and there carved with Ozias' signs to keep them on their way.

"We'd never make it if we had to deal with ice," Jack said, already panting a little. "I thought there'd be ice. There's snow on peaks that aren't as high as this."

"I think we might be on the south side of the mountain by now, or near enough," Ellayne said. "Maybe this part gets too much sun for there to be ice."

Jack thought that sounded like rot, but didn't feel like saying so. There should be snow and ice, but there wasn't—that was all he knew. Anyway, talking made him realize how hard it was to breathe up here. There was something wrong with the air. Breathing it was like drinking weak tea: it didn't quite satisfy.

When you looked up, you could see the trail vanishing into the great cloud. It was like the kind of thick fog that sometimes hung over the river in the early morning. Jack prayed it wouldn't be any worse than that.

"How much longer, do you think, before we're in the cloud?" Ellayne asked. Jack turned to answer her—to snap "How should I know!"—but what he saw, when he turned, made him stop in his tracks.

Below and behind Ellayne he could hardly see anything at all—nothing but a smoky murk that swallowed up the trail they'd just passed over, the nearby mountains, and the sky.

"Well?" said Ellayne.

"Never mind," Jack said. "We're already in it."

Toiling all through the night, Martis feared his strength was almost spent. He plodded on, wasting no extra energy in speech or even thought. He was like a man walking in his sleep—until Dulayl woke him by neighing shrilly.

And the bray of an ass answered him.

It took Martis a moment to remember that the children had a donkey with them. Then he realized that the sky was grey now instead of black, and he could see. Somehow he'd missed daybreak. He really must have been asleep on his feet. But now he was awake, and suddenly filled with fresh strength.

"Hello!" he cried, and that cry echoed and rebounded all around the mountain. He recalled hearing somewhere, sometime, that it was dangerous to raise one's voice while high up on a mountain. He took the echoes as a warning not to do it again.

The ass brayed, Dulayl replied, and Martis pressed on swiftly. In a few moments he came upon a sheltered space where grass grew, and a hobbled donkey wandered from tuft to tuft, feeding. The animal watched him now, twitching its tail and its long ears.

"Is there anyone here?" Martis said, careful not to be too loud.

It was obvious that the children had left the donkey behind and gone on to the summit without it. Martis saw a pile of firewood, the remains of a campfire, and a little heap of baggage, blankets mostly. He knelt by the campfire and felt the ashes with his palm.

Still warm. He'd made good time overnight, and closed most of the gap between himself and the children. They couldn't be very far ahead of him. He sighed.

"We've done it, Dulayl!" he said. "We'll have a drink of water, I'll have a bite of bread, and then I'll catch up to them. I'll be there when they ring the bell—if there is a bell."

He let go of Dulayl's reins and sat beside the fire. He'd lost his own water bag, but the children had left one behind. Very thoughtful of them. When he reached for it, something fiercely jabbed his hand. He snatched it back, thinking only that he'd been bitten by a snake. He saw blood.

But it was not a snake.

A fierce little face with red eyes glared at him, a hairy face with sharp teeth. It belonged to a tiny caricature of a man, that stood on two legs and menaced him with a little sharp stick with his blood on the tip of it.

Such things could not be. They were the stuff of delirium. Nevertheless, there it was. And it hissed and chattered at him.

For the moment, Martis went mad. He cried out and tried to seize the creature, to crush it to death in his hands. Still chattering, it eluded him.

Martis dove for it on his hands and knees, flailed at it, cursed it; but it was too agile for him. Sometime before Martis' fury burned itself out, the creature got away from him altogether—either went into hiding, or simply ceased to exist. By the time Martis came to his senses, gasping for breath on all fours, there was no sign of it. Dulayl and the donkey, meanwhile, had both backed away from him and were now watching him intently from a safe distance.

"There's a curse on every step of this journey," he said to the animals. "But let me be cursed myself if I give it up here!"

He crawled back to the water and quenched his thirst, and had the presence of mind not to drink too much.

"Dulayl! Wait for me here. Make friends with the donkey, and eat your fill of grass. I'm going after those children. And if you see that imp, or whatever it is, stamp it under your hooves."

He found the sign that put him on the trail, and went on without looking back. His hand throbbed where the little fiend had stabbed it.

What—imps, fiends? What superstitious pap was this? And from a man who was the First Prester's intimate! Martis wondered at himself.

But there was no denying that he'd seen the thing, and imaginary beings don't jab a man's hand with a stick.

Martis, with his weariness thrown off like a cloak, strode up the trail. Above him hung the perpetual cloud of Bell Mountain. Inside it somewhere were the two children.

He was to stop them from ringing the bell. "Under no circumstances is that bell to be rung," were Lord Reesh's exact words. It had been a long time since Martis had thought of those words.

He had to catch up to the children before they could ring the bell. "If it is ever to be rung, that decision will be made here, in this office, by me or my successor."

Reesh's words drove him like a whip. He would have been running, had the way not been so steep.

He knew what his master would expect him to do when he found the children. He had his mace with him.

But why was Reesh so frightened? He didn't believe in God. What did he think would happen if the children rang the bell? Why send his assassin to prevent it?

The unanswerable questions chased Martis up the mountain toward the waiting cloud.

CHAPTER 39

How They Came to the Top of the Mountain

Snow crunched under the children's feet. It was hard, frozen snow, and they didn't sink into it—not even to their ankles.

Jack worried about missing signs. You couldn't see them if they were buried under snow. Then again, there wasn't much you could see. The cloud hung heavily. Jack could see Ellayne, who was almost alongside him, and the snow directly under his feet, and whatever rocks and boulders chanced to loom on either side. You could see about five steps ahead and another five back, and that was all. The cloud swallowed up everything else.

"Slower, Jack!" Ellayne hissed at him. "We don't want to walk off a cliff."

"I'm trying to find the next sign," Jack answered.

"What is that?"

Straight ahead rose a low pile of stones. When they were close enough to see it clearly, they realized it was a pile made by human hands. The heavy stone on top was in the shape of a spearhead.

"This must be the sign," Jack said. "See—it's pointed the way we were going."

"They knew the snow would cover any signs they carved into the path," Ellayne said. "King Ozias made sure we could follow him."

Their voices seemed to carry very far indeed. They hadn't spoken loudly, but the empty stillness of the place made it seem so. There was no other sound to be heard, not even a whisper of wind.

They went ahead more slowly, accompanied by the loud crunch-crunch of their footfalls on the frozen snow. They went hand in hand; if the cloud grew any thicker, they might lose each other. Piles of stones guided them. Ellayne thought it would have to be a very big bell for them to be able to find it at all. Jack wondered if there was still a world outside the cloud.

And there stood King Ozias' bell.

They almost walked into it before they saw it. There it was. Jack had never seen a bell before, but there was nothing else that this could be.

It hung on a chain, supported by a framework of timbers planted in the rock. Ozias' men must have scraped away the snow and chiseled holes in the rock to receive the timbers. You wouldn't think wood could last so long; but these timbers were sheathed in some kind of green metal and wrapped in iron bands.

The bell itself was not the gigantic artifact Jack had always imagined it would be. It was a metal cup but little bigger than his head. Brass, probably, although the metal was too discolored to tell. And from the inside of the cup dangled a rusty chain.

"Don't touch anything," Ellayne whispered.

"How are we going to ring it if we don't touch anything?" Jack said. "We have to pull the chain, don't we?"

"But it might fall apart! It's so old. Let's have a good look at it first."

They stood under the bell and looked up. Inside it was a chain, and attached to the chain was an iron ball. That was the clapper, Ellayne said. "You pull the chain back and forth, and the ball makes the bell ring by banging against it."

"Do you really think it might fall apart?"

"I don't know! I'm sure the wood must be rotten."

Jack stepped back. It all looked solid enough, but he knew about rotten wood. He wouldn't want to be standing under that frame if it collapsed. But they'd have to stand under it if they meant to ring the bell.

"We have to do what we came here to do," he said. "At least try."

"Can we do it together?"

He smiled at her. "It'd be a shame for us not to, I guess."

They stepped back under the bell. Jack took a deep breath of the thin air. The whole mountain lay in silence.

They reached for the chain.

And a man's voice roared at them, "Stop!"

Martis scrambled up the trail as fast as he dared—which was much faster than Jack and Ellayne had climbed it. With every step he made up ground, sometimes losing his balance and dropping to all fours. He clutched at the cold, hard rock until he tore his hands, and kept going.

He knew now what Lord Reesh was afraid of. All the prophets spoke of it. The Lord said He would crush the kingdom of Obann; and to be sure, the kingdom was no more. But that was two thousand years ago. There was no more kingdom to be crushed.

Greater than the kingdom, as the noonday sun is greater than the faintest star, was the Empire; and the ruins of the Empire were a thousand years old. Martis knew the Scriptures well enough to know that if the kingdom of Obann had displeased God, the Empire must have infuriated Him. So some scholars taught that the awful day of the Lord's wrath, proclaimed by all the prophets, applied to the destruction of the Empire—a far greater and more thorough destruction than the destruction of the kingdom.

And what would be a greater and more terrible destruction than the destruction of the Empire?

Surely the destruction of the whole world: and that was why the First Prester had sent his assassin to kill a pair of peasant children. Martis understood it now.

He hated Reesh for believing in God and pretending not to, and teaching others not to. "For teaching me not to!" Martis growled through his teeth. For these lies he'd been chased by giant birds. Had Reesh not believed in God, he would not have feared the bell. He would not have believed in the bell, either, and Martis would never have had to make this accursed journey.

He was still cursing his master when he became aware that he'd entered the cloud and was all alone in it. Bent low, he saw tracks in the snow—the children's tracks. Licking his chapped lips, he pressed on, following their tracks.

He must have been going faster than he thought, because when he looked up again, he saw two small figures standing underneath a structure that supported a hanging bell. The sight froze him in his place.

"Stop!" he cried; and he reached for his mace.

Ellayne did stop, but Jack looked over his shoulder and saw a man approaching them. The cloud hid his features and the details of his dress. He might have been a ghost. All Jack knew was that this man, whatever he was, meant to stop them from ringing the bell.

"Now, Ellayne!" he cried, and reached again for the chain.

Ellayne didn't fail him. Together they seized the chain, and their bare skin stuck to it.

And they pulled.

The bell began to move. They tugged on the chain. The iron clapper struck the bell. And Jack, who had never heard a bell before, heard this bell peal.

The first sound was only a clank; but as they set the bell in motion, it began to toll as a bell should. Jack had expected the sound to be overwhelming, even shattering, as it was in his dream. But Ozias' bell brought forth a rich, mellow tone, sweet and pure and powerful, and it echoed among all the neighboring mountains hidden by the cloud. It was a wonderful, glorious, musical sound.

Jack caught a glimpse of Ellayne's face. She smiled radiantly, and tears poured from her eyes. He felt tears freezing on his cheeks. The bell was in a rhythm now, and it took no effort to keep on tolling it.

Martis dropped to his knees and clapped his hands to his ears, and tried to drown out the tolling of the bell by screaming over it. But each knell was a hammer blow that fell on him, the sound of the world being hammered into fragments. He screamed, but no one heard him. He couldn't even hear himself. The bird's beak gaped to swallow him.

The song of the bell played around the mountaintops, and traveled downward.

On the slopes of the mountain, just at the tree line, Obst heard the bell as he lay dying. He smiled in his sleep.

Instead of dying, he got up. He picked up his staff, tied a water bag to his belt, and began to walk back down the mountain, with the sweetest sound he had ever heard ringing in his ears and filling all the space among the mountains. The thought of Jack and Ellayne never entered his head. All he knew was that he had preaching to do, a great deal of it. He'd be a hermit no more.

The song rolled past him down the slope, even as the sun began to rise above the mountains.

East of the mountains, it roused Heathen warriors to mill about their camps in wild surmise. Not knowing the Scriptures, they had no understanding of this strange event, and they were afraid.

In the forested hills, birds woke and sang in response to the song of Bell Mountain. Deer and bear and wolves lifted up their heads and raised their voices, not knowing why.

Trappers and hunters crawled out of their shelters, and settlers emerged from their cabins, all amazed that they should hear a bell tolling in the wilderness.

The song flowed over the plains. Helki and Jandra woke. The little girl, who had never learned to read and never visited a chamber house, recited Scripture. So did Helki. They couldn't hear each other; they could hear nothing but that marvelous music that seemed to come from every direction at once. The sun peeked over the mountains, and they rejoiced.

The song rolled on. In Lintum Forest, Latt Squint-eye fell out of his bed and cursed the terrible noise, not knowing if it meant an earthquake or a storm that would uproot every tree.

Along the Imperial River, boatmen and dockworkers and lumbermen woke and scrambled out into the dawn, staring this way and that, seeing nothing that could account for the tolling of a great bell. Many feared it, but a few felt something in their hearts that was like a release from the worst trouble they had ever known.

In the town of Ninneburky, Ashrof sat up in his cot and knew at once why he was hearing the sound of a bell in a town that had no bell. He sat huddled in his ragged bedclothes, shivering with more than cold; but whether it was fear, or inexpressible joy, he could not say.

Across town, Ellayne's mother and father woke at the same instant, each filled with a sudden conviction that their daughter, who was lost and for whom they mourned, was not lost and had not died, and their whole house and their bed vibrated in response to the loud tolling that had awakened them. They held each other tightly, and Ellayne's mother wept for joy. The chief councilor tried not to cry, but in the end, he did.

The song flowed on. In the great city of Obann, crowds filled the streets and people looked up in wonderment at the bell towers. There were many bells in Obann, but not a single one of them stirred; and yet the whole city was filled with the sound of a great bell tolling.

In his private bedchamber, Lord Reesh heard the sound, knew that his assassin had failed, and fainted dead away.

The tolling of Ozias' bell woke trappers camped in the mires and bayous where the great river ran to meet the sea. And all along the coasts, fleets of white gulls took to the air, flying in tight circles over the waves, calling raucously as gulls do.

The song rang out over the seas, and the islands in the sea, and through lands and peoples unknown to the scholars of Obann. In less time than it takes to tell, the song of the mountain pealed to the ends of the world and back again. There was no place where it was not heard.

And then it ended.

Jack and Ellayne had no more strength in their arms. They stood, panting, looking up at the bell. Jack was sure he saw cracks running all over it. And he saw something else, too: the frame that supported it began to sway. Only just in time, he grabbed Ellayne's arm and hastily stepped back, pulling her with him. And the timbers parted, one from the other, and collapsed; and King Ozias' bell broke into several pieces.

Except for the sound of their heartbeats, silence reigned—until Ellayne spoke.

"Do you think God heard it?" she said.

Jack nodded. "If He can hear us when we whisper, then He must have heard the bell. I hope so. It wasn't as loud as it was in my dream—nowhere near."

But then a breeze blew up, and swirled around the mountaintop, and chilled their cheeks. It scooped up snow and made a screen of it, so that now the children couldn't even see the fallen timbers two steps in front of them. The breeze swelled into a wind, and whistled in their ears. Grains of ice pelted their lips. Terrified of being blown right off the mountain, they dropped to their knees and held on to one another. They had to close their eyes, or have ice driven into them.

This is the end, Jack thought. The mountain's going to fall down. God heard the bell, and it means the end of the world.

Just as his face began to go numb, the wind stopped—just stopped. He imagined he felt sunshine on his forehead.

"Oh, Jack! Look!"

Ellayne jumped up. Jack opened his eyes.

"There's no more cloud!" she cried. "It blew away! Look—you can see everything!"

Jack stood up and looked. At the same time, miles and miles away, men and women and children, Temple and Heathen, looked up and wondered what had happened to the cloud upon Bell Mountain. For the first time since people started keeping track of time, the bare peak gleamed under the morning sun against a bright blue sky.

But Jack and Ellayne looked down, not up; and that worn-out, weary world that was like a dirty carpet, that world that they'd looked down on so many times on their way up—that world was changed.

"What happened?" Jack said. "The colors are so bright!"

The grey plains were now an emerald green, the steely grey river a shimmering blue. The forests that had yesterday looked like old scum piled on a stagnant pond, today bloomed lustily in more shades of green than Jack had words for, and bright red where the trees were just coming into bloom.

They were too high up to see people or animals or even towns, but if this was truly the same world they'd left behind when they entered the great cloud, it had since received a very thorough cleaning, buffed and washed and polished till it shone.

"It looks new," Jack said.

Martis swooned before the bell stopped ringing. It was as if he fell into a black pit and just kept on falling and falling, forever.

Now he opened his eyes. He lay on solid ground, falling no more, with one side of his face pressed into snow and the other side receiving sunshine. The effect was so strange that it blew the panic and the madness out of his head. He pushed himself up with his hands and looked around.

He saw that the bell was down, its supporting framework ruined. He saw the children pointing this way and that, and heard them chattering excitedly about a new world. He saw that he could see now: the cloud was gone.

His first thought was that he'd failed in his mission. They'd rung the bell, and it would never ring again. He'd failed to stop them. If he ever returned to Obann, Reesh's new assassin would kill him.

And his second thought was this: "Everything Reesh taught me was a lie." All those people he'd killed, all the hard missions he'd completed—probably those people should have been left alive and those missions left undone.

His whole body ached, and he stood up with a sigh. The children wheeled, and saw him.

"Who are you?" the boy demanded.

Martis laughed. "You don't know what you're asking me, young sir! But to answer you briefly, the Temple sent me to make sure you didn't ring the bell. I was sent to kill you. But you needn't reach for your knife. I won't hurt you now—or ever."

"Why should we believe you?"

"Because I can't stop you from ringing the bell, now that you've rung it. Because the man who sent me on this mission was a liar. And because I doubt very much that God would let me hurt you."

Jack and Ellayne stared at the man from the Temple. Ellayne recognized the Temple insignia on his torn, stained coat. Jack thought the man looked ill—or maybe just worn out close to the point of death.

"If it's any help to you," Martis said, "I've followed you all the way from Ninneburky. I know your names are Jack and Ellayne. I met a man named Helki, who saved my life. I met your friend, the hermit, Obst, and parted from him in friendship. I'd very much like to see him and talk to him again, if he's still alive. It was Obst who taught me how to read the signs, so I could find you."

Jack and Ellayne exchanged a look. Obst! In all the excitement, they'd forgotten him.

"We want to see him, too," Ellayne said, "more than anything in the world."

"Then we've got to go back down the mountain," Jack said. "There's nothing more for us to do up here. We've done it!"

They all went down together.

This is the end of the story of how Jack and Ellayne climbed the mountain and rang King Ozias' bell. When they came down from the mountain, of course, they had many more adventures. But these are told elsewhere.